Red Dirt Rocker

by

Jody French

A Division of Neverland Publishing Company
Miami, Florida

This book is a novel and contains fictitious elements. Some names, characters, places, and incidents either are products of the author's imagination or are used fictitiously. Some events and names relating to actual locales or persons, living or dead, either are fictitious or are used by permission.

Cover Photo by Athena Rainbolt

Cover Design by Joe Font

Library of Congress Control Number: 2012935485

Printed in the United States of America

ISBN-13: 978-0-9826971-39

www.neverlandpublishing.com

You came last but not least, my blue eyed son,
Leaving your mark with the songs that you've sung

With a rambunctious scream, or a soft church whisper,
Honor and faith lead your steps that are so sure

With golden spun curls, a cherub on Earth,
God sent us an angel the day of your birth

Of the stars in the night, you're the brightest one...
My lion, my lamb, my blue eyed son

From "My Children's Eyes" by Jody French

For my beautiful children, Jessica, Skylar and Forrest
You are the music in my life~~

PROLOGUE

It was a cheery Friday afternoon at Coweta Central Elementary. The first, second, and third graders filed into the musty gym that smelled like lunch. The school was hosting the student talent show, and excitement filled the macaroni and cheese and cinnamon roll scented air. High-pitched chatter bounced off the old stone walls of the gymnasium and mingled with the shrill voice of the music teacher, Mrs. Hall, as she commanded the students to quiet down, sit still, and to put their hands in proper places.

Tutus, tap shoes and trumpets punctuated the bleachers. A very pretty, petite girl sat straight, with a sparkling tiara nestled in her golden, spiral curls. Most of the students didn't think that being a beauty queen should be considered a talent, but

Heather had been crowned "Little Miss Fall Festival" in October, and wanted to show off her fancy dress and ornate crown. Her planned performance was minimal, though. Little Miss Fall Festival would be demonstrating how to perform the perfect pageant wave.

Principle Shrievport's strong voice came across the static of the P.A. system. *Ksssshhh* "Attention, Tiger Cubs. Today is a very special day for our elementary students. Some of you will be showcasing your talents. Let's all stand and recite our Tiger Cub Creed before we begin."

Forrest, a second grader in Mrs. Phillips' class, was especially excited about the show. He was going to get to play his electric guitar for the first time in front of his friends. Forrest stood with a serious face and puffed his chest out with pride. The sweet, innocent voices of the elementary school munchkins began in unison,

"We are students at Central Elementary and this is our pledge:

We will not use the words, 'I cannot do it.'
We will say, 'I can try' instead.
We are each a bright possibility.
Showing respect and honesty,
We will handle the day with positivity.
We are Tiger Cubs at Central Elementary!"

The children finished with a rambunctious roar. They were brought back to order, and seated by Mrs. Hall as she announced her welcome to the parents.

The first act up was a first grader, Bobby Jackson. He wore a grey, flat-top hat and plaid knickers that made him look like Oliver Twist. Bobby sang, quite off key, "Just a Spoonful of Sugar," from the movie *Mary Poppins*. Some of the children snickered as they squirmed on the dusty gym floor, not at all impressed by his squeaky vocals. Mrs. Hall encouraged the scattered applause as she commended Bobby on a job well done.

"Next we have Forrest French, who will be playing his little guitar for us," Mrs. Hall announced, in a slightly patronizing tone.

Forrest climbed down the bleachers, propelling himself off of the last two steps. His heart was beating fast, not because he was scared—his heart always seemed to beat fast when he played his guitar. He grabbed his brand new, maple finish Gibson from a stand near the stage and hopped up onto the platform, not showing the least amount of nervousness. Forrest's blonde hair was spiked into a spunky Mohawk, and his smile revealed the empty space where his two front teeth had been just one week before.

The student body continued to fidget as Forrest plugged in his amp. Static sputtered once again from the P.A. system. As Mr. Shrievport yawned, the mini-musician unleashed his metal fury. The young crowd jumped, along with Principle Shrievport, as Forrest began to play, note for note, solos and all, Metallica's "Enter Sandman." His little fingers moved fluently over the strings as he bobbed his head to the rhythm of the driving tune. The students' mouths dropped open and they began to whisper and shake their heads in approval of the mysterious heavy metal riffs. The faculty and parents also watched and listened in shock. Forrest plucked the last note that rang out in a long, perfectly toned whine, and then faded.

You could have heard a pin drop for a few seconds, and then wild cheers and applause began. Forrest exposed his toothless grin and flashed the rock sign to his new found fans. It was exhilarating. Forrest's mother, Lilly, who was also his roadie for the day, wore a wide, that's-my-baby, smile.

Mrs. Hall stepped back to the mic, but was almost unable to speak. She adjusted the collar of her turtleneck as though it had suddenly gotten warmer in the gym, cleared her throat, and nervously continued. The microphone squealed loudly. Mrs. Hall looked like a chicken pecking grain as she bobbled her head back and forth until the mic finally behaved.

"Uh-um...Thank you very much, Forrest. That was *incredible*...a-a-mazing!" she stuttered. Mrs. Hall regained her composure and announced the next contestant. "Okay, now, let's move on. Our next act is Little Miss Fall Festival, Heather Stevens. Heather will be demonstrating the art of being a beauty queen." Several short critics throughout the audience moaned in disappointment. Forrest was a tough act to follow, but Heather glowed with confidence and poise. She twirled in her frilly frock, showing off her sparkling rhinestone crown and exposing her perfectly starched, ruffled pantaloons beneath her dress.

Heather demonstrated how beauty queens should wave in a parade as Forrest replaced his electric guitar into its stand. Before he could get seated under the basketball goal on the floor, a wrinkly scrap of notebook paper and a broken purple crayon were passed over to him by a fellow first grader, who looked up at him with a carbon copy toothless smile, and asked the young musician to sign his very first autograph!

CHAPTER ONE

Seven o'clock sharp and the shrill alarm of my Superman clock can't be ignored. I whack the top of the Man of Steel's head to silence the dreaded beeping and reach blindly for my cell phone. Yep, I'm a typical teen—my BlackBerry is my lifeline.

I type in my first text of the day with bat-like precision, not even looking at the keys. The message: **Hey u guys awake? ya need a ride?** I send it to my girlfriend, Heather, and my best bud, Kyle. Their responses: **Yes Babe, I'll b ready in an hour**, sent from Heather, and **No, thanx man...dads runnin' me in...My truck'll b out of the shop tomorrow. See ya at school!**

"Okay," I tell myself, "If Heather and Kyle can rise and shine, so can I."

My two fellow night owls had stayed up with me until after midnight, chatting online about the latest YouTube videos. If I was this tired, they had to be dragging as well. I groan and stretch, feeling a dull soreness all through my body. Football practice had been grueling yesterday. I feel like I'm bruised all over—like the muscles in my shoulders and thighs are connected by short rubber bands.

"No pain...no gain," I mumble to myself as I press my feet on the chilled, creaking, oak wood floor. A stark coldness starts at my feet and travels to my brain. I'm finally up and at em'.

My morning ritual always begins with a heartfelt greeting to my well-polished guitars hanging on the bedroom wall. "Hello Ladies," I yawn and greet the axes, patting my favorite, a Les Paul beauty I named Betty. She's my very first expensive guitar. Betty is a looker, with a gorgeous, warm, maple finish and a shiny black fret board. Mama and Dad saved up all year and surprised me on my sixth birthday with the Gibson six-string. I will treasure her forever.

All of my nine guitars hold a special place in my heart. Small squares of soft felt cloth and bottles of special cleaning solutions litter my TV stand and desk—a speck of dust can't be found on any of my babies!

I grab my iPod and plug it into the homing device stationed in the bathroom. Dave Grohl and The Foo Fighters' growling vocals and driving sound will help motivate me for the busy day ahead. My sister Megan and I share the hall bath, but it's more suited to her décor. Mauve colored wall paper printed with tiny baskets of flowers, gilded cherubs on shelves, and bottles of every Bath and Body Works scent that was ever formulated clutter the counter space. Mama has hung an old, vintage, Led Zeppelin t-shirt on the door with a fancy Victorian hanger, which I think, was her attempt to help masculine the place up a bit for me.

Surveying my face in the mirror, I can't help but be proud of the slight, fuzzy shadow growing on my chin. My teammates and I decided not to shave for the month of October, as well as November. After two weeks, I've given up on the hope of more substantial facial hair, but still think I look at least a year older. Thanks to outdoor football practice, I still have a tan. Mama says it seems to make my blue eyes glow. When I was little, I thought my eyes did get bluer in the summer—Megan still teases me about that one.

I scratch my scalp and shake my unruly blonde, curly hair. I've been accused of looking like a surfer dude, but I'm no California beach bum. Stepping back from the steamy mirror, I strike a stance with an imaginary guitar in hand and grimace as I play a silent, thrashing riff to the Foo Fighters song, "Pretender," that's blaring in the background. I jump, my heart thumps, and my "all in" air guitar performance is sadly interrupted by a hard knock on the bathroom door.

"Forrest, get a move on or you're gonna be

late...and turn down that music for Pete's sake!" my dad, Tom, yells through the door.

"Sorry, Dad," I call out over the music. Turning the volume down is one of my biggest pet peeves. It always bums me out, and let's just say my dad is certainly not a big fan of loud.

"Good luck at the game tonight, bud. I'll see you at the stadium. Oh, and Mom got you some vitamins." Dad's voice trails off down the hallway.

"Bye, Dad...thanks!" I shake my wild, snake-like, Medusa hair one more time before jumping into the shower. The pounding jets and hissing steam soothe my aching muscles. I reach for the gold Dial soap, alias my microphone, and continue my a.m. solo, karaoke jam session.

After a half warm, half freezing cold shower, thanks to my sister Megan hogging up most of the hot water, I throw on my faded grey Levis and Metallica t-shirt and grab my bulky backpack. I'm still humming the Foo Fighters' tune as I make my way to the kitchen. Mama is fixing my standard weekday morning breakfast—toast with chunky peanut butter and a tall glass of milk that she always puts in the freezer for five minutes to make it icy cold. She's also laid out two horse-choking vitamins and a water bottle on the counter.

"Good moorrning honeeey," Mama sings out. "Please remember to take your vitamins. Between football and band practice, you're burning the candle at both ends. I want to keep my baby boy healthy," she says thoughtfully.

Mama's precious comment isn't lost on Megan. "Yeah, Mama's baby boooooeeeyyy!" My sarcastic sis mocks in a Flava-Flave like rapper tone.

"Well, she didn't offer you any vitamins, so I guess she loves me more!" I open my mouth, which is full of well chewed up, gooey peanut butter. I know it will completely gross her out.

"Yuck!" Megan squeals, turning her head so quickly that a strand of her jet black dyed hair flings around and gets stuck in the corner of her mouth. "Your truck better not be parked behind me this morning or you're gonna have some major fender damage," she lectures coolly.

"No, I didn't park behind you, but watch out for the mail-box on your way out," I return with a whine, knowing I'm getting her goat. I down my entire glass of frosty milk in four big gulps, let out an award winning belch, and kiss Mama smack dab on the cheek.

Mama shakes her head, "Thank you soo much, son."

Megan continues to protest. "Oh, my *gosh*! Will I *ever* live that one down? It was just a small ding—the sun was in my eyes. It was *not* my fault!"

I love to rib Megan every chance I get, but we're still very close. We have each other's back if needed for sure. There's not much difference between our ages. Megan is eighteen and I—drum roll please—am sixteen and a half and driving! We're only one grade apart in school. Megan is a senior and I'm a junior. Secretly I know I'm going to miss Megan when she goes off to college. She's been a 4.0 student each and every year and front runner for Valedictorian of her class. I'm very proud of my sis, but would never, ever, even under Chinese water torture, admit it to her.

My best friend, Kyle, is graduating this year, too. I sure dread the changes. I don't know what I'll do without my best buddy and my older sis. Kyle's my confidant—I love him like a brother, and I'll sure miss giving Megan a hard time on a minute-by-minute basis. I know I'll be able to call Kyle anytime, day or night, and I figure I can always text my daily comic insults to Megan long distance, thanks to our AT&T family plan.

"You two be careful," Mama orders, as Megan and I suddenly begin a jostling footrace for the door to the garage.

"No worries, Mama. I'll go set some orange construction cones out on the driveway...that way Megan won't smash into the mailbox again," I tease as I grab onto her backpack strap and spin her around three hundred and sixty degrees.

"Forrreeesst!" Megan hollers. She grabs my t-shirt and knocks my flat-billed Batman cap down over my eyes as we jockey for position in the door frame. I win by squeezing through first.

Ahhhhh, sibling rivalry.

CHAPTER TWO

As I toss my musty football bag into the bed of my Chevy, I can feel the nagging tightness in my shoulder from yesterday's tackling drills. I gently place my guitar case in the back of the cab and seatbelt it in like a child.

My white-with-blue-interior 2002 pickup truck is my pride and joy. I paid for it by teaching guitar lessons for the past two summers and quickly learned that when you have to pay for something yourself, you definitely appreciate it more. I understand now why Dad always nags me to turn off the lights, or why Mom gets discouraged if I pour too much milk and end up wasting half a glass. My truck may not be the newest model on the road, but it sports a killer speaker system with bass that can thump. I love my truck.

I pull into the street behind Megan and give her an annoying and unnecessary honk. She holds up her thumb and index finger in the shape of an "L" to signify that I'm a loser. She rolls her eyes at me and guns the engine of her measly four-cylinder Chevy Cavalier. I give her a peace sign and a goofy, sarcastic grin as I fly past her on a stretch of open road.

The early sky looks like rainbow sherbet with whipped cream clouds glowing in pink, orange and yellow heavenly hues. I yawn as I gaze at the inspiring color of the morning. I'm reminded of God's power of creation and fall into a mini daydream as I stare at the heavens above.

Time to get the old juices flowing. I return my concentration to the road and plug my iPod into the converter in my dash. This time the members of the Zac Brown Band are the rock stars of my truck cab concert. Their raspy, smooth, southern sound fills the air and makes me happy.

I pass six cars, and in five of them I know the drivers and their families by first and last name, as my hometown isn't much larger than a peanut. Coweta, Oklahoma, population six thousand. My friends and I call it "Cow-Town." Our small town has more dirt roads than highways, more barb wire than city lights. Ranchers outnumber doctors and lawyers, and I wouldn't have it any other way.

After driving four more blocks, I spot Heather standing at the edge of her gravel driveway. She's a picture of self-confidence, the type of girl that relishes the second looks she gets from the motorists passing by. I swear, where most girls would blush at the unsolicited attention, she tends to lean into the whistles and cat calls without a hint of embarrassment. Heather knows she's a total hottie.

Heather's silky chestnut brown hair always has the perfect part, her bright, jade-green eyes are mesmerizing…they're what first drew me in. She also has amazing legs that look killer in a cheerleading skirt. Today is assembly day at school and she gets to wear her uniform and show those legs off.

Heather's skirt is at least an inch shorter than those of the other girls on the squad. She said it was an accidental alteration, and since she's the team captain, there's no one higher in rank to give her a hard time.

"Good mornin', good lookin," I greet Heather, as I throw open the rusting passenger door. Heather grabs the "oh crap" handle, pulls herself in, and slides over next to me. She adjusts her polyester skirt and dumps her lead-heavy, hot pink Hurley backpack on the floorboard. Our oversized textbooks make our backpacks feel like we're carrying around a small toddler on our backs all day.

Heather looks at me with a slight hint of agitation. "Why did you have to get a truck? It is sooo hard to get in and out of. Did you see D.J.'s new car? It's a brand new Honda Civic, all pimped out. You know…the shiny black one?"

"Yeah, yeah. I saw it yesterday." I say without interest. "I like my truck. I can go muddin' on the back roads, and haul hay for my Aunt Carmen in this baby," I respond, as I pat the warm, slightly cracked leather dashboard affectionately.

"Whatever," Heather dismisses. She grabs me by the arm and cuddles into my sore ribs like a purring kitten. "Can you pleeease turn the music down a little bit?" she asks, rubbing her temples, I believe, in an attempt to fake a headache.

"That's twice already this morning," I mumble.

"What, babe?" Heather asks, as she surveys her perfect manicure. Each fingernail is embossed with a tiny orange and black tiger paw. I wonder how girls think of these things.

"Oh, nothin.' "Your hair looks nice," I compliment.

Heather smiles and kisses me on the cheek. Her good mood returns with my flattering words. "You're a living doll, Forrest," she beams as she pulls my rearview mirror down to her eye level. She strokes her perfectly straightened, highlighted hair and reapplies her powder.

I reach up to wipe her finger smudges off my mirror. Sometimes I think Heather bases her good days and bad days on how many compliments she gets. This was compliment number two, if you count the honk she got from the farmer in the one ton truck earlier, and it wasn't even 8:30 a.m. yet—her day is probably shaping up nicely already.

I make a right onto Broadway. It's the second day of October and most of the small, worn houses that line the street are already decorated in the

Halloween spirit. Hay bales, pumpkins and strung up spider webs make for creepy, quaint curb appeal.

My brakes squeal slightly as I come to a stop in front of Sticky Buns Doughnut Shop. Heather has to have her morning cappuccino. As I enter the small coffee and sugar scented shop, I hear two elderly women whispering rather loudly. I wonder why they're bothering to whisper at all, since everyone within a twenty foot radius can hear them—the donut shop is probably only a hundred square feet altogether.

The two women have strategically positioned themselves at a table directly by the door so that no one can escape their fastidious inspection. A black velvet painting of a tabby cat with huge, green, exaggerated eyes hangs above them.

They continue to cluck away and their conversation unfortunately drifts along with me as I make my way to the orange and gold chipped linoleum counter.

"Oh, Thelma, I knooow! Ruth Walton has not been widowed for more than eight months and she is *already* holding hands with John Franklin in church at Sunday service!" one of the ladies clucks. Her wrinkled, thin, painted-on ruby lips are pursed together as though she has just sucked on a sour lemon slice.

"It's just *scandalous*!" The other blue-haired patron of the pastry shop agrees. She turns up her nose and shakes her head under hair that is piled high in a perfectly pinned, bluish silver bun.

Well, I happen to know Ruth Walton, and wish the two women would mind their own business. Mrs. Walton lost her husband to a long bout with cancer almost a year ago. She found a companion in John Franklin, who's an elder in my church. He'd also been widowed years earlier. They're both very sweet, kind-hearted souls who deserve continued happiness.

I purchase a sugar-free vanilla cappuccino and two maple bars and try to make a clean getaway from the two gossiping hens. As I pull on the door to exit the shop, the dangling brass cowbell that is wired to the top of the door clanks loudly above me. It draws attention to my departure and I know instinctively, as the two women eye me carefully up and down, that I'll be their next topic of conversation.

My long, shaggy, Peter Frampton-ish hair is certainly not the norm for our small, conservative town. I don't know why I look back. Maybe I'm just hoping that I really do fit in, that it's just my imagination and the two ladies are back to sipping their coffee and nibbling at their apple fritters, but as I glance back over my shoulder, I notice one of the women pointing at my wallet chain. I'm sure the two busy-bodies think I whip it around in gang fights, but the heavy metal chain really has a valid use—it keeps my wallet from being stolen in a crowd by anchoring it securely in my back pocket—great for concerts.

The tips of my ears begin to warm and tingle,

and are doing the proverbial burning from gossip, as I jump back into my truck. I hand Heather the steaming, frothy drink and fire up the engine. She's changed the dial to a country station while I was inside. The radio is playing a song by Miranda Lambert called, "Famous in a Small Town." It's a clever country tune that tells the story of gossip in a little town and how it can make some of its town folk "famous" in a not-so-good way.

I think to myself, as Heather and I drive down the jack-o-lantern ridden main street of our one-horse town, Mrs. Ruth Walton and I are definitely on our way to becoming celebrities this morning.

CHAPTER THREE

The halls of Coweta High School are buzzing with the festive mood that game day always brings. Tiger spirit is thick in the air. Orange and black butcher paper banners with big white shoe polish letters are hung, declaring, "The Tigers are gonna leash the Bulldogs!"

I find it kind of odd that me and my fellow football players are treated like heroes in both our school and community. We're warriors of our small town, with many fans pinning their hopes and dreams on the promise of a winning season. Depending on the prestige of our position on the football team, we might score anything from on-the-house burgers and fries from the local Snack Shack to free tokens for car washes at the Country Suds Car Wash. It's awesome, though—I'm always lucky enough to end up with a full stomach and a clean, shiny truck.

As I make my way down the rowdy hallway, I give three high fives and receive two good luck nods from my fellow Coweta Tigers teammates. I come to a stop when I reach my locker and take a long breath. Unfortunately, I have a bottom locker this year and have to do squats every time I need to open it. Squats are okay in football, but not cool in a busy hallway.

As I dig through the disorganized mess inside, Kyle sneaks up on me from behind, giving me a hard shove on the rear that knocks me off balance. I fall face-first into a mass of notebooks and loose-leaf papers.

"Duuuude!" I yell. My voice echoes as I pry my head from the rectangular metal box. With wide eyes, I turn to see my evil buddy holding his stomach. He's having a great laugh at my expense.

"Who'd ya think gave you the love tap...old Mrs. Smith maybe?" Kyle asks, cackling. Mrs. Smith teaches history. She's fifty-two years old and is unfortunately taken—married for the past thirty-four years, to be exact.

I don't skip a beat. "No! I thought it was your *mama*, Kyle!" I retort sarcastically.

"Ohhhh, that's sooo wrong!" Kyle moans with a tone of defeat. He grabs his chest as though he's been physically wounded. The score is now one to zip. Victory is mine for the battle of the wits this morning.

"Hey, ya' ready for the game tonight?" Kyle asks as he helps me retrieve the notebooks and crumbled papers that had shot out of my crammed locker like birthday confetti.

"Yeah, but Coach has been killin' us. I'm still gimpin' from practice yesterday," I complain as I stretch and rub the back of my stiff neck.

"Man, I know...but it'll all be worth it when we thump the Bulldogs tonight," Kyle agrees. His sympathy is short-lived, however, and he punches me squarely on my aching shoulder. "Try not to be such a girl! See ya at lunch, dude!" my best friend adds with an ornery grin as he hands me a handful of papers imprinted with dusty tennis shoe prints.

Kyle and I are off to class. We join the herd as we dive into the swiftly moving river of students, accompanied by the sound of clanging orange-lacquered lockers.

Besides playing football, my other passion is jamming in a rad, teen rock band called Cellar Door Is Gone. We play classic rock, along with our original stuff, loud and tight. My first hour at school is with my bandmates. I get such a kick out of them. They are *total* dudes.

I dodge a whole fleet of white paper airplanes as I walk through the door of Mrs. Smith's classroom. I'm glad I scored her as a teacher this year. She smells like tea roses and reminds me of my Nana. Everyone likes her because she doesn't give homework and never refuses a bathroom pass.

I'm enveloped by the stuffy, floral-scented air as

I greet the boys in my band with our secret handshake and fist bump. I spot Jake, our cool-as-a-breeze lead guitarist, at Mrs. Smith's desk, working on a hall pass, even though the tardy bell hasn't even rung yet.

"Hey Forrest, did ya get the show scheduled for Saturday in Tulsa?" asks our drummer, Cody. Cody is quiet and unassuming. He's got a shy smile that throws people off. His sandpaper sense of humor is dry—his random one-liners always crack me up.

"Yep, I sure did. We go on at nine o'clock...we can take the gear in my truck. My aunt's driving, too, so if any of you wants a girlfriend to go, she's welcome to ride with her," I offer.

"What girlfriends?" Randy, our band's bass player whines. "Duuude, you're the only one with a girlfriend right now," he continues, as he carefully folds his past due English homework into the shape of a fighter jet.

"What about the hot chick you said you've been talkin' to for the past two weeks?" I inquire with a wink in Cody's direction.

"On-line girlfriends don't count, man," Cody teases.

"Hey, I'm gonna meet her someday...I can't help it if she lives in Canada!" Randy responds defensively.

"Ummm...any ideas on how you're magically gonna become six feet two with abs of steel...not too smart sending 'cyber-girl' a picture of the captain of the basketball team, Einstein," Cody continues.

"Hey! I'm startin' a workout routine." Randy defends earnestly as he launches his stealthy folded airplane at Cody, nailing him right in the nose. He immediately regrets the decision. "Oh, shoot, give that back, dude. I have to turn that in next hour," Randy pleads in vain.

As Randy tries to retrieve his homework from Cody, who's holding the half-finished book report/Boeing 747 above his head out of his reach, I begin to think how awesome it would be to have a girlfriend who would actually come hear me play. I know Heather won't be coming to my show. She attended one of our concerts a week after she and I started dating, but complained that it just wasn't her cup of tea—the music was too loud. I told her I understood, but deep down I wish she liked the same music as me.

"Dang, I'm hungry," Randy grumbles, rubbing his chubby stomach. "I'm gonna get a bathroom pass and hit the vending machines by the teacher's lounge. You losers want anything?" he asks as he checks his Hot Topic hoodie pocket for loose change. He finds fifty cents in dimes and nickels, and begins scraping lint-covered, green spearmint gum off of one of the coins.

"You just sat down, dude!" I laugh. "It's only eight thirty in the morning."

"I know man, but all I had for breakfast was an Egg McMuffin and sausage biscuit from Mickey D's—I'm ready for dessert," Randy reasons with a straight-as-an-arrow face. I swear, I can almost see two Snickers bars shining in Randy's eyes like cherries in a slot machine.

I slap Randy on the shoulder, slide down in my seat and begin to work on my history worksheet. I'll more than likely have to share my answers with my bandmates, mostly because I have a solid "A" in the subject. Jake, Randy and Cody are currently pulling C-minuses, thanks to my generous homework sharing. They're on their own for the history tests, although most of the time they just write the answers on their hands or Scotch tape them to the bottom of their high-tops and Van's.

The tardy bell rings and the classroom gets quiet. I look one row over at my good friend Zane who looks especially zoned out this morning. I notice the dark, haunting circles under his eyes and I send him a text message on the down low.

We got the gig in Tulsa!!! you can ride with me if you want to go-is everything ok at home?

Zane sneaks his cell phone out of his jeans pocket and scans the text. He nods to me with his chin, declaring that this is a good thing as I survey his eyes as best I can behind the veil of long, fine black hair that usually hides his expressions.

The bell rings for second hour. As the classroom begins to empty, I lean into Zane. "See ya at lunch man." I can sense Zane's melancholy mood as he gives me a thumbs up and tries to muster a semi-smile. *His step-dad must have started in on him already this morning*, I think to myself.

I exit the classroom, and shake my head as I

hear Randy's voice in the distance asking what's on the lunch menu today.

The last hour of my dragging school day finally arrives. Heather and I walk arm-in-arm to the gymnasium for the pep assembly. PDA is discouraged at school, so I give her a quick hug as the Tiger marching band begins to file by in Noah's Ark fashion, two by two. Heather stands in front of the trophy case, admiring herself and adjusting her skirt in the reflective glass. Her gaze is interrupted when a clumsy trumpet player, deep in conversation about the movie *Tron*, accidentally bumps into her.

"Hey…watch where you're going, *nerd*!" she yelps loudly.

"Wow, Heather—a bit harsh," I scold under my breath.

"Forrest, he could've snagged my cheerleading uniform. He needs to get his glasses checked," she replies while brushing imaginary cooties off her polyester cheer top.

"Well, first off, he wasn't wearing glasses," I point out. I have no other words. I just turn and walk away, feeling a sense of discomfort and guilt by association.

If she weren't so gorgeous…surely she's just having a bad day, my thoughts excuse her behavior for now.

As I trot across the gym to take my place with my buddies on the football team, I look down at the free-shot line to see two drum sticks rolling toward my worn, black Converse tennis shoes.

"I'm sorry!" a petite and very cute drummer girl squeaks. She tries in vain to retrieve the sticks in the crowd, but her bulky, oversized, fuzzy band hat keeps getting in the way.

"Here ya go," I say proudly, as I pick up the sticks and spin one in my left hand. The drummer girl thanks me, giving me one of the sweetest smiles I swear I've ever seen.

"You'd better hurry. I really need to get my spirit up for the big game tonight," I tease, pointing to her fellow bandmates who have already assembled and are warming up with random squeaks and squawks on their instruments.

We both hesitate for a second, staring into each other's almost matching blue eyes.

What a dad gum cutie!

"Thanks again," she says nervously, wringing her fingers together. She grabs the sticks and disappears quickly into the stands.

"Wow...she's adorable," I state out loud to myself, the airy words from my mouth getting lost in the noise of the packed gym.

The pep assembly is rowdy and fun. Heather is the prettiest girl on the cheerleading squad, and is droppin' it like it's hot to a censored Snoop Dog jam. She's definitely the center of attention as she swings her shiny pony tail, cascading from an oversized orange bow, back and forth like a well-kept show horse at the Muskogee County Fair. She and D.J., the football team's quarterback, lead the assembly. As the students, jammed against each other in the bleachers, cheer with them, it's obvious that Heather and D.J. both relish the spotlight.

After the assembly, D.J. boldly tells Heather that she looks totally hot in her cheerleader uniform. That was her third compliment in the last seven hours. As I watch Heather giggle and flirt with D.J., I can't help but think that his forward comment is probably making her day.

CHAPTER FOUR

It's perfect fall weather. Not too hot and not too cold. The air feels crisp and cool. Dad would say it's the kind of day where you could just smell football in the air. My dad can always smell football in the air. He even has a leather-scented air freshener in his truck, which I'm sure is to make it smell like a brand new football—not a new car.

Dad was a jock back in his day, too. He's very proud of my athletic ability, and never hesitates to encourage me in anything sports-related. He coached my peewee baseball and football teams and literally never missed a game. I remember the first time Dad helped me put all my equipment on when I was six years old. It was like trying to go out to play in the snow after your mom bundles you up excessively. I was so excited, but could barely move my arms and legs, and looked like a bug with my huge helmet on my little noggin. It's something you get used to eventually, once you realize your pads and helmet are your lifesavers.

Like Dad, my favorite sport was football. By middle school, I quit baseball, as I'd discovered that the two extracurricular activities that made me happiest were football and music. Now I'm a starting linebacker for my high school team and, on occasion, get to step in for D.J. as quarterback. I love leading the team as quarterback, but I know for a fact that D.J. becomes resentful when I take over his position.

D.J. and I used to be good friends when we were in grade school, but he later considered all of life to be a competition. If you were beating him in any part of the game, he was more than likely not going to be your friend.

My buddies tell me that D.J. is also jealous of the fact that I'm going out with the most popular girl on the cheer squad. He has his eye on Heather, which creates the perfect recipe for tension soup.

It's a game day, so football practice is light. Kyle and I make our way out onto the field in shorts and practice jerseys—no pads needed—there will be no full contact during practice today.

As I walk by D.J., he just can't resist the chance to rib me like he usually does.

"Kyle, are you and your lady friend ready for the game tonight?" D.J. snickers.

I turn to face him and D.J. retracts. "Oh, I'm sorry

Forrest. Your hair is gettin' so long, I thought you were one of the water girls...niiiiiice!"

"That's really original, D.J.," I respond in a monotone. I don't want to give him the satisfaction of a rise, but I'm getting tired of his cheap shots.

"Oh, come on, rock star...I'm just teasin' ya... where's your sense of humor?"

D.J. laughs as he jogs by. I'm not amused in the least, and I can tell by Kyle's face, neither is he.

"Don't worry about him, Forrest. D.J.'s got issues. Probably wasn't cuddled enough by his mommy when he was a baby," Kyle remarks dryly.

"Ah, good one!" I grin as we slap a high five in front of D.J. Now I can tell it's D.J. who's not amused.

The team is on the fifty-yard line, walking through some special team plays, when I toss Kyle the football. It's a perfect rotating spiral. I can't help but admire the launched football as it torpedoes its way sixty yards through the clear blue sky. Kyle jumps vertically two feet. His sure hands catch the pigskin and firmly cradle it into his chest. He holds the ball over his head and hoops it up. "Yeah baby!" he declares proudly. It was a good throw, but an even better catch.

Kyle is a wide receiver on the Tiger team and an excellent athlete. The coaches think he has a good chance of being recruited to play at one of Oklahoma's universities. He's a dedicated player with good hands and lightning speed. I'm proud to call Kyle my teammate, and my best bud.

We've been friends since we were toddlers. Our parents met when we were still in Pull-ups. We even got to share a birthday party in pre-school. Believe it or not, it was a John Deere tractor party. John Deere is the equivalent of Mercedes Benz in our small town, so it made Kyle and me feel like big-time farmers. We got to go to my Aunt Carmen's farm and ride on the green and yellow combine tractor that had an air conditioner and cassette player. A Kenny Rogers tape played "You Picked a Fine Time to Leave Me Lucille" as Kyle and I made a couple of rounds in the soybean field. Mama still displays the framed picture of Kyle and me decked out in our overalls, holding our little toy tractors. We've shared a lot of fun memories. I'm sure we'll be friends for life.

Kyle and I continue to play catch and talk about our upcoming game. I can see D.J., and the team's center, Sam, whispering and elbowing each other. They look like they are up to no good, and are mysteriously pointing in our direction.

Sam is D.J's "yes" man. He'll do almost anything that D.J. dares him to do. His nickname is "Box," because he's built like a sturdy square—just as wide as he is tall. He weighs around 275, and is only five and a half feet tall. He's not the sharpest tool in the shed, but he can sure hold the line. Box is a massive, dull-witted beast!

Kyle throws me back a bomb and I stretch for the pass that's just a bit too far over my head. Out of the corner of my eye I can see Box barreling towards me like a charging bull. His fat arms wrap around my waist and both my feet lift off the ground. I feel like a helpless rag doll as he makes his blindside tackle.

Everything seems to be moving in slow motion. I hold my left hand out to catch myself and wrench my wrist into the dry turf. It takes me a few seconds to realize what has just happened. Knots build up quickly in my gut.

Box stands up and brushes himself off. His fat rolls ooze out of the bottom of his jersey, like flesh-colored Jell-O. D.J. stands off to the side, with his head cocked back, laughing hysterically.

"*What* the *heck*!" Kyle wails as he sprints over to my defense. I grab my wrist. My heart skips a beat. *Okay, it's not broken*, I think, relieved, as I survey the movement in my joints.

Kyle grabs for my good hand and steadies me back onto my cleats. I glare at D.J. and Sam with clenched teeth, my jaw muscles pulsing with anger.

"*What were you thinking*? Why did you hit me, you freakin' idiot?" I growl, holding my arm to my side. "How stupid can you be? I didn't even see you coming, dude," I fume.

"Oh, Forrest. Box didn't mean to hurt ya. Can't ya take a joke?" D.J. sings out sarcastically. "Just let your boyfriend Kyle comfort you."

"Not a funny joke!" Having said that, Kyle then lunges at them, kicking up the orange clay so it drifts their way.

"It's all right, man. I'm okay, Kyle." I assure him as I

try to collect my thoughts. I knot Kyle's jersey between my fingers and pull him back. He's acting like a frenzied-but-tethered pit bull.

The coaches blow the whistle signifying the end of practice. What I really want to do at this moment is to let Kyle go in for the kill, but quickly decide it's not worth a fight, and I sure don't want Kyle to get kicked off the team for punching Box or D.J. I have to convince Kyle to head back to the field house without popping one of them in the mouth first.

"Man, Forrest...D.J.'s a jealous jerk. We shoulda' whipped em' right there on the field," Kyle says, spitting angrily on the chalked sidelines.

"Naw. I'm okay. I know D.J. dared Box to tackle me—we all know that Sam's a few bricks shy of a load anyway. It did kinda freak me out when I fell on my wrist, though. My band would kill me if I couldn't play my guitar at the show tomorrow, and my dad would totally freak if I missed the game tonight," I reply, stretching my left arm out in front of me. I know I'm letting them off the hook, but as long as no major damage was done, I'm relieved.

I still fight to control my anger before it gets the best of me. Kyle chunks his cleats in his stale gym locker and slams it shut with a vibrating clang.

"Dang scum-suckin' jerks!" he huffs. "They'd better watch their step, is all I have ta say."

I shower quickly and leave the field house. I have a couple of hours before the game and need to clear my head. I have to keep my cool about the tackling incident because I don't want Kyle to jeopardize his position on the team by fighting, but inside my blood is boiling. I have to leave quickly before I say or do something I might regret.

I was taught that fighting isn't the way to solve my problems. I'm not a fighter, although out on the field, I sure wanted to take a piece out of D.J. For now, I take solace in the fact that D.J. will pay for his jealousy and ignorance someday. Life has a way of taking care of bullies, and D.J. is an insecure loser.

I jump in my pickup, gun the engine and head west on Highway 51-B. I turn on my stereo, roll the windows down, and let the sweet country air swirl into the cab and clear my head.

Focusing on the barbed wired fences that I'm driving alongside, I begin to think how they remind me of the rugged, barbed wire tattoos that I've seen on so many of my rock heroes. I'm not sure what God thinks of tattoos. I've always imagined that if I ever got one, it would be okay with the Man Upstairs, cause I would get my favorite Bible verse permanently inked on my skin: Philippians 4:13. "I can do all things through Christ who strengthens me." A pair of rugged praying hands would make it just perfect, I envision.

Right now I need strength to be able to hold my temper, and not tear into D.J. I need to go to my practice place and play my guitar. Playing guitar is my form of meditation. It always helps me think calmly and clearly.

I continue down the dry, bumpy country lane lined with tall oak and paper-shell pecan trees.

Lengths of light filter through the branch canopy above the road. A reddish-brown trail spins behind my truck like a dusty ghost. Parking in front of an old red barn, I lean back in the seat, close my eyes and ask for self-control. I slap the steering wheel with my good hand, sling open the creaking Chevy door, and step out into the wide-open countryside. I'm at my home away from home—I'm at Aunt Carmen's farm.

CHAPTER FIVE

My favorite place in the whole countryside is our practice headquarters for the band—an old, weathered barn that has been faithfully sitting on Aunt Carmen's acreage for over fifty years. The barn also houses her quarter horse, Mojo, five farm cats, a goat named Gotcher, (as in "got yer goat"), dozens of field mice, and even a wise old owl that takes shelter in the hay loft. It also stores all of my band's music gear.

Aunt Carmen's place is a country paradise, with just the right balance of boot-scootin' charm and modern luxuries. I often come here to ride Mojo and just chill.

There's a swimming pool behind the large stone and brick house that a mother duck and her ducklings consider their own private, oversized bird bath. They have a large pond, but leftover corn bread thrown out the back door keeps the feathered friends coming back for more.

The inside of the house is warm and inviting. Aunt Carmen's kitchen has brick floors and a big, black potbelly stove. It looks like an antique, but it's actually an induction oven. Great Grandma Nellie's recipes have been handed down to Mama and Aunt Carmen. Grandma's old-fashioned fried chicken and apple pie are still the specialties of the house.

I start for the old red barn and hear Aunt Carmen's voice echoing from the front porch. "Hey, Forrest, honey! Would ya please put Mojo out ta pasture before you boys start yer band practice? I gotta meatloaf in the oven—you'll need somethin' ta eat before yer game tonight. Come on in after yer done playin,' sweetie!" she calls out with a thick southern drawl.

"You got it, Aunt Carmen. Thank you, Ma'am," I call back to her. My mouth begins to water at the comforting thought of Aunt C's savory tomato-sauce-topped meatloaf and the fluffy, buttery mashed potatoes that always accompany it.

I pry open the splintered barn door and, as usual, the skittish barn cats shoot out like supersonic fuzz balls over my Sketchers. They jet across the yard to the front porch of the main house. Mollie, the family dog, a chunky black Lab that is old and half blind, tries in vain to catch up to one of the wild kittens. It's not that Mollie would harm the feline—it would be more like she would lick it to death. There's always a lot of good, old-fashioned hospitality at the farm.

"Come on, Mojo boy," I say as I pat the large beast on his meaty hindquarters. Dust bunnies fly up and swirl in the golden late afternoon sunlight. Mojo is a slick, red sorrel Quarter Horse gelding. I recall wanting to know what a gelding was several years ago, but when I got the answer, I wished I hadn't asked. Let's just say poor Mojo won't be making any Mojo Juniors!

"We gotta jam, old boy—you'll be better off in the pasture till sunset." I open the black iron gate that leads to 40 acres of fertile pasture land and a serene pond loaded with sunny perch. After unfastening the lead rope from Mojo's halter, I watch the liberated beast trot off. His head shakes proudly from side to side. Mojo's coarse, flowing mane flies, burning like flames being fed by the wind.

I smile and think to myself, as I watch the powerful animal pick up speed when he reaches the open field, *That's how I feel when I play my guitar—FREE!*

I pull my well-worn guitar case from the back seat of my truck and make my way back to the musty, but weather-tight, barn. A bass amp, two Marshall amps, a mic stand and a gold chrome Gretch drum kit take up the north side of the building. This Jam Barn is the official practice headquarters for my band, Cellar Door Is Gone.

I open my leather guitar case that's plastered with faded band stickers and pull out my other pride and joy, Betty, my Les Paul sweetheart. Betty is nestled securely against the tattered, red, crushed-velvet case lining. I slip my guitar strap, imprinted with smiling skulls with blue glowing eyes, around my neck. I take a deep breath. Exhaling, I begin my much needed escape.

As I reach down to plug in the cord that runs from my guitar to the amp, I'm grateful for the blank-slate feeling that washes over me. I begin to play a random melody. I think of nothing. I close my eyes and see a symphony of color. I let my calloused fingers strum the yielding metal strings. The confusion that has previously filled my head is replaced by feelings of peace and pure joy. My heart beats strong—I feel in control. No matter what has taken place during the day, or how discouraging life seems to be at the time, I can always count on the power of music to wash it all away. Nothing compares—not video games, not sports, not even girls. Music is my saving grace—music is my true love.

I drift into a song that my band and I had written earlier in the year called "Sweet Goodbye." My band buds and I have been playing together for five years now. We got together at the ripe old age of eleven. Jake and I heard each other play during our fifth grade talent show. He and I had both started playing guitar at a very early age. Mama raised me on classic rock music, and Jake's family tree was full of southern country rebels who loved to rock, as well.

We needed a drummer and learned that Cody was taking lessons. He lived just a bike ride away. Cody thought he would have to beg his parents to let him move his drum set to Aunt Carmen's barn, but that wasn't the case. They were more than grateful for the peace and quiet.

We talked Randy into playing bass for us because he lived just one homestead over and wore awesome vintage concert t-shirts to school. He may have started with us because he lived close by and looked cool, but we kept him with us because he had incredible rhythm and could slap a bass.

Aunt Carmen says our band is as organic as the horse manure in her south forty. I think that means that it all came together in a very natural way. We decided on our band's name after high speed winds forced me and the boys into the farm's root cellar one stormy afternoon. We were practicing when Aunt Carmen came busting through the barn door. She had a sense of urgency on her face, and ordered us to follow her while maintaining a controlled panic.

As we ran across the farmyard, I noticed the sky had turned a sickly grey-green color. Hail the size of quarters began pelting us. I spotted Mollie trying to squeeze through the lattice under the front porch and sprinted to pick her up. Aunt Carmen screamed for me to let her be, but I just couldn't. I grabbed Mollie, soaking my shirt with the skunky smell of wet dog, and jogged back to the shelter. I handed her down to the other boys as she grunted and groaned from arthritis. I then insisted that Aunt Carmen climb down the steep rickety steps before me.

As I held the door open for her, the hail stopped. It was as if someone had flipped a switch and blackness came. It became eerily calm. I started my descent down the cellar stairs. It was like a scene from a nightmare. I looked up to see the wicked side-winding twister that had emerged from the ominous squall line. The door fell shut with a sharp crack and we all huddled together in the darkness. The smell of garden onions and dusty potatoes was thick in the humid air.

Next came the sound...the forbidding sound that only a tornado makes. A growling, rumbling, whistling sound as though the 10:00 Frisco freight train had been diverted directly across the top of the root cellar door and was ready to fall in on top of us.

We were all paralyzed with fear as the twister roared over like an angry monster. I've never felt so small, so scared, so close to God. Aunt Carmen held the boys and me in her motherly arms and prayed out loud to Jesus. Dirt and wood splinters spun violently over our heads and it sounded like someone cracking open a pop-top can. The sucking winds ripped the door off the root cellar, but we didn't budge. It was all over in a matter of two terrifying minutes. The untamed twister disappeared back into the dark and thick rolling clouds.

Jake was the first to go back up. The boys and I hoisted Mollie up the stairs brigade-style. We expected to see a war zone as we emerged from our bunker, but to our shock and relief, the tornado hadn't done much damage to the barn or the house. They were both left virtually unscathed. The only things the twister took with it were an old rusty plow, two black shutters from the house, and the creaky wooden door to the root cellar.

The boys and I stood in disbelief as we surveyed the property. All the color had drained from Cody's face. He repeated over and over, "The cellar door is gone…the cellar door is gone."

"Cellar Door Is Gone...that's it...that's our band's name," I said in no more than a whisper. The hair on our arms seemed to practically stand up and shout, "Yes!" The boys heard me loud and clear.

The sun began to peek back out from behind the smeared, grey clouds. The cold drops of rain dissipated. Wispy chicken feathers, or perhaps bits of the snowy down of angel wings that protected us that day, swirled around our tennis shoes. My band brothers and I shook our heads in agreement—Cellar Door Is Gone it was.

CHAPTER SIX

I continue to play our band's original song, "Sweet Goodbye." I wrote the song with D.J. as my inspiration. It's about changing relationships, and the unfortunate fading of some friendships over time.

My friendship with D.J. sadly ended years before. He and I used to play kickball on the playground every day in elementary school, but it all ended in third grade when D.J. and I got placed on the same baseball team. He wanted to play first base, and it became my position. D.J. was our pitcher and did a great job, but his competitive nature got the best of him at our second game of the season.

I was the only leftie on our team and panicked when my glove mysteriously disappeared from the dugout just minutes before the beginning of the first inning. My dad gave me his right hand glove and sent me out to center field. D.J. was put at first base and I had to play the rest of the game as a right hander. We lost the game and D.J.'s dad found my left handed ball glove in D.J.'s baseball bag. He insisted he didn't put it there, but our short stop admitted he saw him slide it in before the game started. D.J.'s dad took him out to the parking lot by his ear and grounded him from his Play Station for two weeks. D.J. ignored me on the playground from that day on.

D.J. is an incredible athlete and sly as a fox. He always *yes sir* and *yes ma'ams* his coaches and teachers, but I know his true colors. He still deals with me as though I'm his competition, not his friend.

I'm bummed that D.J. feels this way, but grateful for my bandmates, and especially Kyle. We have an unconditional friendship that will last. There's nothing I can do to erase the resentment that D.J. feels toward me, so I feed off the "friendship gone sour" story, and channel my feelings into my songs.

I first started writing music for the band when I was just twelve years old. My juvenile and corny compositions started with the typical themes of rock star dreams, lyrics about our amps, guitars and the beat of the drums. As I continued playing and experiencing life, the quality of my songs matured. I could sit down in a single night, if the feeling inspired me, and write an entire song, lyrics, melody and all.

Song writing had become my passion. I could transform my hopes, dreams and conflicts into musical form. Mama said it was a gift—a gift that cost me nothing to share.

I close my eyes and I begin to sing:

Life will not be the same without you
I'll never doubt you
But you turned away from me
I just wanna forget about you
Sit out on a bayou
And sing you a sweet goodbye

As I play and sing, I become distracted by a tiny barn mouse that's scurried out from under a hay bale. I sit for a second, watching the tiny, dusty grey rodent nibble on a piece of Mojo's molasses coated sweet feed that has spilled out onto the barn floor.

I think to myself, *What a simple life the barn mouse must live—no school, no cell phones, no computers, no girlfriends, no chores…might be nice.*

The mouse darts back under the hay bale and my daydream is interrupted as a motley crew bursts through the barn door. It's my bandmates.

"I found some hitchhikers on the road!" my sister Megan announces as she heads the pack.

"Dude! Were you really hitching?" I question, shaking my head. (I find myself shaking my head at my bandmates quite often.)

"Yeah, we were hangin' at my house after

school and didn't wanna wait for a ride, so we just hit the open road. Ya know, when you're carrying a guitar case, people think you're legit," Jake boasts cooly.

"Well, looks to me like my sister was the only one that thought you looked legit. You guys are insane." I chuckle. "You're lucky a serial killer didn't pick you up."

"I'm outta here, guys," Megan waves. "And *no* more stickin' your thumbs out," she lectures, pointing her motherly index finger at the boys.

Jake, Randy and Cody thank Megan for the ride. She exits the barn, leaving the scent of her Cotton Candy Bath and Body Works spray behind.

"Man, she smells righteous! Just like sugar cookies," Randy mumbles with a dreamy expression floating across his round baby-face.

"Yeah, your sister's *hot*!" Jake declares, and Cody nods heavily in agreement.

"Oh Lord, pleeease do not *ever* say that in my presence again!" I beg with my hands over my ears.

"Sorry man, but if the skirt fits..." Cody adds dryly.

"Oh forget it, guys," I concede as I approach the mic stand with my head dropped in denial. "Let's just play!"

I wait for Cody's cue to start the first song. He always clicks his drumsticks four times to begin our jam session, but only silence fills the large barn. All the boys hesitate, standing motionless at their designated jamming stations. I survey the stoic expressions on their faces and I can tell they have something on their minds. The boys never do "serious."

Jake is the first to pipe up. "Hey, Forrest, we heard in sixth hour that ya got hurt, or maybe broke your arm in football practice today." He begins with concern.

"No, no, not broken. My wrist is just a little bit sprained. D.J. had his brain-dead sidekick Box tackle me without pads on when I wasn't ready for it," I explain, hoping to squelch their worries.

"Man, Forrest, you need to be careful. Ya know that D.J. has it in for ya. He freakin' *loves* Heather. He's been jealous of you guys since the first day of school," Jake continues as he reaches down to connect his frayed and duct-taped guitar cord.

"Yeah, Forrest. What if you break your arm or somethin' and can't play your guitar? We really wish you'd quit football," Cody adds, as he instinctively twirls his sticks.

"It'll be all right, guys. Don't worry about a thing. Besides, my dad would disown me if I quit the team now. We're havin' a winning season. It looks like we might actually have a chance for the playoffs. It'll all work out," I assure them. The only problem is, I'm not even quite convinced myself.

"Okay, man...if you say so, dude. Yeah, it'll all work out. Just be careful, man," Jake finishes, putting an end to the serious discussion.

After a few seconds of uncomfortable silence, Randy mumbles. "Hey, Forrest, ya know what?"

"What?" I respond cautiously.

"Chicken butt!" Randy answers matter-of-factly. "Ya know why?" He questions with a smile.

"Chicken thigh!" I grin widely, thankful for Randy's random joke.

Jake and Randy raise their guitars to their hips. "Let's rock this mother!" Cody exclaims, as he cracks his wooden sticks four times and crashes his cymbals.

We light right into our original song, "Rocket." It's a totally catchy hard rock tune that some would affectionately refer to as an "ear worm," a song in which the chorus gets stuck in your head and you can't help but hum it all day long once you've heard it. This is maddening to some, but magic to record labels.

As our music reverberates off the dry, splintered barn walls, it's very apparent to me that my buds and I were born to make music—music that will stick in people's heads for a long, long time.

CHAPTER SEVEN

I'm revived and ready to go after the mini jam session. Playing guitar always helps to clear my head and ease my mind, and Jake, Randy and Cody never fail to make me laugh.

I think about my bandmates and their very warranted concerns. I secretly wish I could channel Superman's powers as I continued to juggle my family time, social life, football, and my band. I don't want to let anyone down. School...check, band practice...check. Now it's time for football—hut-hut!

I pull up to the field house and can see that Tiger Field is buzzing with activity. Hundreds of cars line the parking lot, and spill over into three acres of open field. The home stands are already packed with loyal fans. It's Friday night and the high school football game is the place to be. There isn't much else to do in town, so there's always a standing-room-only crowd of loyal supporters.

I take a deep breath and enter the testosterone-filled locker room. All of my teammates' voices automatically lower a few octaves as we talk major smack about our chicken-livered opponents. We put on our armor and prepare for battle.

I charge onto the dewy field with my fellow soldiers as the marching band fires up the fight song. The blast of the trumpets and the pounding of the drums is our war call.

I look to the steel bleachers and find my family in their reserved seats just below the press box. It gives me strength and comfort to see them there and feel their support. I know come rain, shine, sleet or snow, they'll always be there for me. Hearing their cheers gives me an extra push. Mom and Dad wave wildly at me as I jog onto the wet, green, glistening turf. I pause at the giant air brushed tiger head painted at the center of the fifty yard line, slap myself in the helmet then sprint to the sidelines.

"Go get em,' Fooreest...LET'S SEE SOME GOOD HITS!" Dad booms. He's in his element, enthusiastically coaching from his seat every game. Mama said it gives him an adrenaline rush to watch me on the field. Anyone can tell that it's the highlight of his blue collar, or should I say, "brown collar," UPS work week.

It's kick-off time. The fans rally us on with clanking cowbells and homemade noise makers. Water bottles filled with gravel rattle the home stands. My team goes into attack mode.

Our game is close at half time, but we pull ahead after the third quarter, with a final score of twenty-seven to seven. The coaches pull D.J. out and let me guide the Tigers for the last three minutes of the game, where I connect a forty-yard pass with Kyle for the last touchdown. I can tell from his expression that D.J. is always angered when I step in for him. Quarterback is his position, and he doesn't want me calling the shots.

My teammates and I celebrate the team's victory, but D.J. is busy sneering.

The Tiger marching band plays "Go Big Orange" on repeat as Heather comes bounding up to me in front of the field house.

"Forrest!" she squeals, jumping up and down. "You all *won*! Let's go celebrate, sweetie!"

"Hey, Heather," I huff, still out of breath. I try to greet her with a warm, sweaty hug.

"Eeewww!" she yells, pushing me away. "Go take a shower and I'll wait for you—you stink! There's a big party at D.J.'s house tonight. He even has an awesome hot tub," she quips, matter-of-factly.

"Heather, to be honest," I hesitate, "I'm dog tired and really just wanna go home, put some ice on my wrist, and maybe watch a movie. Does that sound ok?" I don't have to wait for her answer. I already know what it's going to be.

"Now, Forrest, I am the head cheerleader. What would it look like if I didn't attend the after-party? Really, you need to think about that," Heather returns. She swirls her curly, glossy ponytail between her fingers, trying her best to look bright-eyed and innocent as the bossy words roll off her tongue.

"Heather, why don't you go on to the party without me? I'll text ya in a bit. I'm not really up for a major celebration tonight," I reason.

I sure don't want to go to D.J.'s. I know what after-parties consist of—a keg, smoke, and a lot of my friends doing things that I know they wouldn't normally do under sober circumstances. It just makes me feel awkward and uncomfortable. Being straight-edge means I make the decision not to drink or smoke. It seems ironic to me that these days, being a straight-edge teen means you're considered a rebel of sorts—the odd man out.

I did go to one beer bust after our first game of the season. My buddy, Zane, talked me into driving him out to a cow pasture on Ben Lumpkin Road where they were having a kegger to celebrate the win. I became the "D.D.," or designated driver. Well, within twenty minutes, the alarm was sounded. The cops were on their way! I helped snuff out the puny bonfire and the party was over. I led the pack, driving my Chevy like the *Dukes of Hazzard*, bumping and skidding through the field like a bat out of Hell.

Zane had somehow managed to chug nine beers in less than thirty minutes and was already totally blitzed. As we high-tailed it out of the pasture, Zane let out a belch that registered on the Richter scale and began to mumble in a Captain Kirk-like voice.

"Forressss...youuu...are...my besss friend. I been drinkin'...but I'm saaaafe. I'm t-o-t-a-l-l-y waaasted, dude. And...you're drivin' me tooo safety. I loooove ya, man!!!"

I then had to pull over to let The Zane-anator upchuck in the ditch. Yep...good times!

I don't want to go hang out at D.J.'s house, and I know Heather is clued in to that. She's beginning to show her true personality, which makes her suddenly not so attractive to me.

"Okay, party pooper. I'll talk to ya later," Heather says, pouting. She glances behind her and suddenly decides to give me a big hug, sweat and all. I'm pretty sure her public display of affection is intended to make D.J. jealous. It works. The cranky quarterback rumbles by.

"Get a room!" D.J. mutters sarcastically.

I'm not too surprised when Heather doesn't get offended by the remark. She just giggles and pushes me away quickly.

"Tootles, Forrest. Text me later, doll! Hey, D.J, wait up!" she yells, dismissing me with a wave of her perfectly manicured hand.

I really can care less where she goes or who she goes with at this point. I'm now just hoping to find the right time to break up with her. She is most definitely a beautiful girl, but her selfish attitude is wearing me thin.

After my team's rowdy, towel-popping victory celebration in the locker room, which adds two more raspberries to the three I already have from the game, I head home alone. Between my school day, band practice and the football game, I'm beyond exhausted and totally ignore my promise to text Heather. I figure she's too busy partying it up in D.J.'s awesome hot tub, more than likely in her teeniest bikini, to even care.

I put my headphones on and adjust my fat goose-down pillow under my sore neck. I'm exhausted and quickly drift off into a deep sleep as Death Cab for Cutie sings me a lullaby.

CHAPTER EIGHT

The aroma of salty, smoked bacon and pancakes with maple syrup is my favorite thing to wake up to in the morning. To my delight, the warm, comforting, sweet and savory smells drift all the way down the hallway and into my room.

Opening one eye, I decide that the promise of a mouth-watering meal and a tall glass of ice cold milk is worth opening them both at the same time.

I stretch my arm up and rotate my wrist to make sure it's still in working order. I have scabs on both elbows, my back hurts and my neck hurts—my whole body aches from the game last night, but my wrist is my only concern.

I lift my arm toward the ceiling fan, roll my hand around, and breathe a sigh of relief. My arm is okay. I'll be in top form for my band's gig tonight.

Mama knocks on my door and enters with an especially sweet smile on her face.

"Mooorning, Mama," I yawn weakly.

"Hey, sleepyhead. It's already ten o'clock. Are ya' ready to get up and have breakfast? I made your favorite—buttermilk pancakes and bacon," Mama says in a soft tone as she kisses me on the forehead, which is the only part of my body that isn't in pain.

She messes up my curls and tells me that I look just like a cherub in a Renaissance painting. "You're my rock angel," Mama declares lovingly.

"Yes...I *am* an angel. That's for sure," I return teasingly. "Breakfast smells soooo good. Thanks, Mama. I'll be right there," I whisper lazily as I stretch my aching muscles and sing out my last long yawn in a tenor key.

Mama's expression suddenly turns serious. "Hey, sweetie...I need to let you know...umm...I got a call yesterday evening right before your ball game. It was from a guy that'll be coming to your show tonight. His name is Dan Manning. He's with Diamond Records.

"Dan's coming to Tulsa to scout your band! He's heard all the hype, checked out your band's YouTube videos and is very excited to come hear you boys play tonight," Mama explains, her eyes open wide and fill with excitement. "I thought it might break your concentration if I told you right before your football game. I knew you'd need a good night's sleep, so I figured that now was the best time to tell you." Mama laces her fingers together tightly and bites her bottom lip like she always does when she's trying to contain her enthusiasm. I can tell she's hoping I won't be upset at her for withholding such pertinent information.

"Seriously?" I question, in total shock. I suddenly bolt upright. "Dude! That's awesome, Mom! I have to call the guys! They won't believe it!" I feel thrilled and nervous at the same time—"thervous" is what Randy calls it. He says that's how he feels before every Cellar Door Is Gone show.

My heart begins to race. "What an amazing way to wake up!" My thoughts buzz. I suddenly turn completely ADHD. I take three deep, calming breaths, grab my BlackBerry and nervously push speed dial for Jake's number. I blurt out the incredible news. Jake flips totally out, of course, and says he'll call Randy and Cody.

I grab my Mac and make the incredible announcement on my Facebook status. My page blows up. I get fifteen encouraging comments in less than three minutes.

We make plans for my mom and me to meet the boys up at Cody's house at 6:00 sharp. Evening rolls around and, true to form, Jake, Randy and Cody are running late. They tell me to go on ahead. The three incessantly tardy boys will ride with Cody's mom and dad and meet us at the venue in Tulsa.

I hear Cody holler from the bathroom that he's having a bad hair day and is trying to fix it. I know better than that. Cody is famous for jumping out of the shower, running his fingers through his Justin Beiberish hair and *voilá*!

"All right, guys. I'll see ya there. Just slap a beanie on Codyman!" I yell, as I leap off the porch like a seven-year-old. I slide into the passenger seat of my truck. Mama is my chauffeur for the night. She still doesn't trust my driving skills on the busy expressway and truthfully, neither do I.

"To the club, James, chop-chop!" I order, with a bad British accent.

"Excuse me, Rock Star?" Mama corrects.

"Sorry…we can go now, Mom," I grin and salute Mama. I can hardly contain my excitement. The boys and I will be opening for the main act at the historic Cain's Ballroom in downtown Tulsa. This is going to be our biggest show to date. My adrenaline is rushing through me like the Colorado River as we pull up to the grungy, graffiti-ridden back lot of the venue.

I hustle inside to visit with Brad, the stage manager, who always gives me breaks on ticket prices and sometimes even autographed copies of band flyers when I go to concerts there. Just last month he scored me a poster from the one and only Ted Nugent. It was signed, "Good hunting Forrest—my fellow soldier of rock-n-roll!" It is the coolest.

A full twenty minutes passes before the other guys finally arrive.

"Better late than never!" Cody announces, as he and the heavy metal posse march across the wooden parquet floor. His hair is a cool, hot mess. It's plastered vertically into a four-inch Mohawk. He's also added bright red and purple stripes on the spikes.

I shake my head at their tardiness, but *love* Cody's hair. I forgive them for being late, and make a mental note to get them all watches next Christmas.

"Wow! This is soooo rad," Cody's voice echoes, as he surveys the large stage.

"Let's get set up, guys," I direct. The boys and I thank Brad, shake his hand like professionals, and get to work. Our families jump right in. They double as our roadies, helping us carry in the amps, guitars and drum set. Sometimes they get mistaken for the band members as they help lug equipment in. It always floors club owners when they realize Cellar Door Is Gone is made up of fifteen and sixteen-year-olds. They're always very pleasantly surprised by the time we finish the first song of our original set list. We've been told many times that we sound like seasoned professionals. I take great pride in that.

With the equipment in place, I make my way out the backstage door to grab my guitar case from my truck. I look around the quiet parking lot. I can't hide my disappointment from Mama.

"Dad said to tell you 'good luck.' His UPS route was slammed today," she says and gives me a tight hug. We both know that Dad could have made it to the show if he had made an effort. It's unspoken knowledge that he doesn't quite support my dream of being a musician. I'm sure he thinks I should concentrate on more practical things—football, to be exact. Just last week, Mama tried to get him to wear one of my band's t-shirts. Dad just said that it didn't fit right, and opted for his Tigers football tee.

I looked at the labels; they were the exact same size—Hanes large.

CHAPTER NINE

Mama finishes hugging me and grabs my shoulders. "Now go kick butt!" she says firmly, clapping her hands together twice. I'm grateful for her support. She and Aunt Carmen always stand front and center at all my shows. Mama mans the camcorder; Aunt Carmen snaps pictures.

They really get into the shows. I always get tickled at Aunt Carmen. She never quite gets the "devil horns" rocker sign right. She always makes the symbol for "I love you" in sign language by adding her thumb into the equation. Mama and Aunt Carmen are my biggest fans—two cool chicks.

Randy and Cody think it's a drag when their moms come to our shows. Instead of cool concert digs, Randy's mom, who is a third grade school teacher, opts to wear a cardigan or denim shirt with apples on it. Cody's mom is really loud and always says hello to us by singing our band's name out in an operatic tone. I think they're all just great. Heck, the more supporters, the better, and Randy's mom always brings her blue ribbon award-winning chocolate chip pecan cookies to all the shows.

Backstage, I peek out from behind the stale, smoke-infused curtain at the growing crowd. It looks as though at least five hundred people are here, but I still feel loose and confident.

I never really get nervous before a show. Once I play the first note of the first song, I'm usually good to go. It's the same way for me on the football field at the start of a game. One good, dead on, smashing tackle and all the butterflies disappear.

As I survey the crowd, someone catches my eye. It's the cute chick with the runaway drumsticks from our pep assembly. I knew she looked familiar. I remember now seeing her at a couple of our shows. She looks so different without her band uniform topped off with the awkward fuzzy hat.

She's standing in the front row of the crowd tonight. Her bright blonde hair is shining in the house lights. To my surprise she's actually wearing the same t-shirt I am—a grey Led Zeppelin tee—my lucky charm shirt. I'm sure hoping it works its magic tonight with the record label executive. She's cut the collar out of hers, however, and snipped it just right so that it hangs casually off her pretty right shoulder.

I can see that she's wearing a bit more makeup than she does at school. Her black eyeliner is swept up at the corners, giving her beautiful, liquid blue eyes an exotic, cat-like appearance. Her perfect, full lips are shining with clear gloss.

I can't take my eyes off her as she stands with her hand on her hip laughing with a group of her friends. For a moment I lose my train of thought—I'm in full daydream mode as Cody walks up behind me and gooses me in the ribs with his drumsticks.

"Let's go, dude. Let's rock this mother!" He commands, twirling his sticks like mini-batons.

I shake my head and come back to reality. I ask Cody if he knows my mystery girl. He tells me her name is Sophie. I put my head back in the game, whip my Les Paul around like a Wild West gunslinger. I hum Pantera's tune, "Cowboys From Hell," move my fingers across my chest in the shape of a cross, even though I'm not Catholic, and cruise in coolly from stage left.

As the boys and I man our positions, the crowd goes nuts. Stepping up to the mic, I scream my usual, "Are you ready to roooock?" Electricity crackles in the atmosphere around the illuminated stage. The guitar amps squeal. Cody snaps his drumsticks together, beginning what is to be our band's best set ever.

During the show, I'm totally mesmerized by Sophie's presence. I find myself singing and playing to her in the crowd. Her rocking skills are more than impressive. She even knows how to head bang like a pro. Her soft, layered blonde hair gets disheveled as she flings it under the smoky colored lights. She sings every word to each song right along with me. Every time I look her way, I feel like I'm floating over the stage. Our eyes lock several times during the show—there's a definite connection between us.

I'm now sure that I want to get to know Sophie—the girl in the marching band drum line—better. She seems way cool.

After the show, our merch table is a madhouse. T-shirts are being slung around as Jake, Randy, Cody, and I sign autographs and our cheap demo CDs for at least thirty minutes. I usually stay longer than the other boys. They inevitably became antsy and go backstage to sneak cigarettes with the older musicians. I know the boys think it makes them look cool and adult-like, but every time I surprise them in a smoke hole, I have the opposite vision. To me they look like children playing "grown-up."

I had decided early on that I didn't need cigarettes to look cool. Besides, skipping the smoke breaks gives me more time for the fans. I absolutely love visiting with them. If there's even a single warm body waiting at our table, I'll be there.

As the crowd at the table dies down, a Joe Dirt look-alike approaches me for a picture. The fan's girlfriend snaps the shot with her camera phone, and he leans in. "Hey man, I got some weed, dude. You cool? You need a hook up, my man?" the avid rocker whispers on the down low. The sharp smell of alcohol mixes with his words.

I smile wide and give him the usual. "No thanks, man...I got Jesus!"

"Oh cool...cool, man. That's awesome, dude!" he stutters, pumping my hand one last time. "Hey man...that's great! Stay that way! We'll see ya at your next show. Seriously, man, you rocked it!" he returns with nervous sincerity.

"See ya, dude! Thanks soooo much for comin' to the show," I say gratefully, before he retreats back into the smoky shadows.

As unbelievable as it is, on occasion, I'll get approached by adults offering me beer, liquor, marijuana, pills...you name it. I think it's difficult for a lot of the fans to comprehend that I'm just a sixteen-year-old kid, and yes it's just a part of the music lifestyle, but I always have the same response when asked to partake. It's a straight forward answer to a straightforward question. I always give them a very firm handshake and tell them, "No thanks, man...I got Jesus." It's not a judgmental statement or a holier-than-thou attitude. It's just how I feel.

Surprisingly enough, it always warrants respect and a smile from the person offering—even from the most hardcore, tattooed, in-a-smoky-haze musicians. My response is usually a shocker to them, but I think most of the time, they're glad to see a teen refuse what might otherwise dominate a large part of their own life.

The rock world is, I guess, a bit of a backward world, when I think about it. Good grades, going to church, and keeping your nose clean is what normal society pushes, but in the music industry, it doesn't mean a hill of beans. It's a crazy world. But, I don't care if I get called a Jesus freak or not—my faith in God is my rock.

I know one thing—I'm sure glad I don't need drugs or alcohol to perform. I get my high from the music. I get my high from life.

In the midst of all the hustle and bustle at our crowded merch table, I suddenly realize I didn't get a chance to talk to Sophie. I'm sure thinking about her though, and am hoping I'll see her in the hallway at school on Monday. I can thank her for coming to my show. Yep, that'll be my ice-breaker.

I think it's so cool, and yes, a bit flattering, that Sophie loves the music into which I put my heart and soul. A beautiful, shy girl like her that likes to get rowdy to my hard rock music. What a concept...very different from prissy, particular Heather.

After the crowd at our merch table dies down and the last band of the night finishes its set, the partying patrons flood out onto the ballroom parking lot, some still bouncing to the music, some weaving from one too many libations. I'm glad to see lots of taxi cabs lined up at the curb.

Dan Manning, the big shot record exec, makes his way confidently over to the boys and me. The suspense is killing us.

Dan's suntanned face has serious business written all over it as he begins to speak.

"Boys, that was a fantastic show—absolutely

phenomenal. I definitely got to see what all the hype was about," he compliments us, and ignores the annoying buzz coming from the iPhone in his tweed blazer pocket. Dan makes his way down the line, shaking each of our nervous, clammy hands. He takes a step back toward the neon green exit sign. Our hearts begin to sink as he hesitates. He rubs his chiseled chin as if in deep thought.

"Well, young men—I've already made a call to Los Angeles. Our label will be sending you lads a manager next week. His name is Frank Turner. He's a great guy—a pro. He'll get you set up in a local studio here in Tulsa to record your single. We really dig the song "Rocket." I believe that will be the one we want to get to the stations first.

"Frank'll be working on some other projects and appearances for you as well. Good luck, boys—you *are* the real deal! I'm truly impressed," Dan ends earnestly, with a flash of his gleaming, oversized Hollywood smile.

When Dan finishes, Jake, Randy, Cody, and I practically tackle him with an out-of-control group hug. Dan regains his balance and begins to chuckle. He shakes our hands one more time before exiting the club. The music mogul is laughing all the way out the door as he steps out into the black night. The Cain's Ballroom sign glows orange and red above his head like a midnight sun. Dan's phone buzzes once again. This time he picks it up.

"Hey, Frank! I'll give you a shout in the morning. I'm taking the red eye back to L.A.—Yeah, they are amaaazing!" we overhear just as the ballroom door closes behind him.

Randy strips off his shirt and begins running in circles. Jake, Cody and I fall in behind him, also using our shirts as celebratory flags, swinging them over our heads. I guess it's official—my Led Zeppelin tee is good luck!

"I wonder if this is how most rock bands celebrate getting signed?" Mama questions, as she and the other parents stand together in shock. They all begin to laugh, hug and congratulate each other on the band's big break.

Randy suddenly stops in mid-celebration. His baby fat hangs over his Levi's like a doughy muffin. "Hey, let's paaarrrty! Can we order pizza? I'm *staarving*!"

CHAPTER TEN

It's Sunday morning—church day. Even if I have a late show the night before, I almost always find the will to rise and shine for the a.m. service at my hometown Baptist church. My first attendance there was exactly nine days after my birth. I was three weeks old at my dedication and received a blue and white checked baby quilt that Mama still has, and was baptized there at the age of ten. My church is a part of my life that always comforts my soul and helps keep my feet planted firmly on the rich, Choska Bottom soil.

A small stream of cheerful sunlight creeps through my mini blinds, gently warming my puffy eyelids. It had been a very exciting and a very late night. It takes me a minute to realize, as my eyes squint open, that the meeting with Dan had really happened; it wasn't just a dream. My band, Cellar Door Is Gone, is going to be a legitimate, signed band! A big, smile grows over my face and doesn't want to go away.

I roll over when my Superman clock begins to shriek. It's ten a.m—time to rise and try to shine. I slap the alarm and throw a pillow at my bud, Zane, who's snoring in a tiger-striped sleeping bag on my floor. Zane had come knocking at my window at two o'clock in the morning. He spends quite a few nights at my house to avoid the constant, simmering tension in his home.

His mom re-married three years ago and unfortunately, he and his step-dad don't see eye-to-eye on too many issues. Zane's mom tries her best to keep the peace in the family, but Zane is a strong-willed teenager and his step-dad considers him just another mouth to feed. The bigger problem is that his step-dad isn't a fan of working a steady job. Zane refers to him as "Lazy Larry." Larry spends a lot of leisurely time on the couch, playing Zane's X-Box and drinking Budweiser, thanks to Zane's mom, who supports all of them by working full time at Wal-Mart.

Zane finds it impossible to hold his tongue when he's being harassed. When the arguments ensue, he usually just storms out and comes knocking at my door or window. He knows he's always welcome, but it's still tough for him. I can tell that he battles depression and sadness as a result of his dysfunctional home life. Like me, playing music is therapy for Zane—it's an escape from his harsh reality at home. Zane and I jam together every chance we get.

"Hey, lazy," I groan, as the pillow I chuck bounces off Zane's head. "My mom's fixin' a big breakfast and we're goin' to church...why don't you come with us, dude?" I ask, raising my eyebrows persuasively. "I've even got a surprise for ya, man," I continue, hoping that the meal and mystery might entice him into joining us.

"Oh, duuudde...shoot," Zane moans as he stretches. "You're lucky your mom's breakfast smells so good, because that's the only reason I'm gettin' up," he weakly responds. We both get a good laugh at each other's wild, bed-head hair.

After a hearty country breakfast of eggs, biscuits, gravy, and savory sausage, thanks to Aunt Carmen's pig, Elmer—may he rest in hog heaven—we head for church. It's a beautiful Sunday morning. Our spirits are high. We're greeted with smiles and *good mornings* as we step into the foyer of the quaint, red brick Baptist Church.

Following three songs from the hymnal, Brother Aaron steps up to the podium and proclaims, in a warm tone, that I'll be performing special music today. I can sense an air of skepticism among the elders of the church as the announcement is made. I've never before played for the morning service. The congregation only knows me as a teen athlete—a player for the Tiger football team—the linebacker that needs a haircut. They don't know much about my band or the music I love to play, and our small town church is steeped in the old Baptist hymns. Non-traditional music isn't usually the norm for the services. My youth director, however, had encouraged me to come forward and play a song that I had written, along with Zane's help.

I rise from my pew and nudge Zane. "Will ya come with me and help me out with the song?" I whisper. "You know this one," I assure him with confidence.

I'm sure Zane feels put on the spot, but he doesn't want to disagree in front of the expectant congregation, so he makes his way down the aisle beside me with his head dropped.

I can feel the stares of the reserved church elders. Zane and I are dressed in jeans and t-shirts. Zane's jeans are heavily frayed on the front left pocket. I see him self-consciously place his palm over the hole. Our heavy silver wallet chains swing loose by our thighs. The congregation eyes our long, stylishly disheveled hair. My curls are shoulder-length, and Zane's fine black hair hangs like curtains across his face. I've always thought it helped him hide some of the sadness that was so often present in his tired and often bloodshot eyes.

I pick up my Boulder Creek acoustic guitar that I had strategically brought there the day before and hand Zane an extra guitar from the stage. I position my microphone clumsily according to my height. The speakers squeal slightly.

Zane continues to eye me with a "What the heck am I doing up here?" look. The morning sun filters brilliantly through the bright, candy-colored stained glass windows behind us. The radiating rays soak into my shirt and feel like a caring hand on my back.

I clear my dry throat. "Zane and I wrote this song this past year. It's about faith, and knowing that you're never alone if you trust in God. We just wanna thank you for letting us play this morning. Hope you enjoy it," I speak humbly.

"The song is called 'Amen.'"

Zane's eyes light up. He gives me a knowing grin. I begin the song with a slight uneasiness; a question of rejection in my tone. As we continue I can see that any doubts that the elders may have had are beginning to melt away. Even the members of the church who usually zone out, and the ones who just pick at their fingernails for the hour long service, sit up and pay attention to the song. I can tell they are all surprised by the soulful, acoustic melody and the from-the-heart lyrics.

Zane and I finish the last note with a peaceful strum of our guitars. *Amens* and applause break through the reverent silence. Even the strictest elders smile with approval as they nod to each other. I feel goose bumps rise on my arms. The warmth of their acceptance envelopes us. A peaceful, pleased expression spreads across Zane's face.

After the service, my buddy and I are met with

handshakes and pats on the back. Joe the barber even offers his services to us free of charge anytime, as a joke, of course.

My dad is beaming with pride. The congregation has oftentimes given Dad kudos for his son's great tackles or a pass into the end zone at the weekly high school football game. Today, Dad smiles widely, as Jimmy the shade tree mechanic shakes Dad's hand, telling him how much he enjoyed his son's hidden talent.

"What a gem. A singin' linebacker!" Jimmy declares boldly.

I thank Zane for helping me with the song, as Mama hugs him tightly. Tears well up in Zane's soulful eyes. But they are happy tears—tears that don't need to be hidden by his long, rebel locks. Dad gives us each a firm squeeze as well. He announces it's time to head to Aunt Carmen's for fried chicken and Porter peach cobbler.

This is a morning that my good friend Zane and I will surely remember forever.

CHAPTER ELEVEN

It's been an unbelievable week for me and my band buds. Diamond Records made good on their promise to send someone to Oklahoma to manage our band. Frank Turner is a hip, smooth-talkin' dude. His style is "I'm fifty, but dress like I'm twenty." He wears what the other boys and I call "Where's Waldo" scarves, and is a true stereotypical music manager, spouting all the latest teen lingo. He gives us "knuks" all the time and says phrases like, "That's how we roll," "That's money, baby," and "Turn up the tuneage!"

The boys and I think his antics are on the verge of corny, but he's a good fit for us. We're still in disbelief half the time that someone from L.A. is actually in Cow-Town giving us professional guidance. Frank set up studio time for our band to make a professional CD with several of our original songs. The recording process is very exciting and educational. We learn how to mix and over-dub. We're able to record three demo tracks in two weeks. In under a month, our first single, "Rocket," is distributed not only to radio stations around the U.S., but is also getting radio play in several foreign countries, as well.

We quickly learn what the term "royalties" means, and it doesn't have anything to do with the Queen of England. It's a term for the nickels and dimes that we earn each and every time one of our songs is played on a radio station, airplane, or even the juke box at our local Dew-Drop-In.

Frank says the label is hoping our song will become a bullet—not the kind of bullet shot out of a twenty-two by local deer hunters, but a single that shoots up quickly on the Billboard music charts.

Frank also lets us know that our management is in talks with the Dallas Cowboys football franchise. Cellar Door Is Gone might actually get the chance to play at half-time for an NFL game! The boys and I are really stoked. Even my dad is excited—he's a *huge* Dallas Cowboys fan. We all feel like we're in the middle of an Oklahoma twister—a rock-n-roll whirlwind.

On the normal side of my teen life, I finally get the chance to talk to Sophie in the middle of the school week. We bump into each other in the hallway between classes and my heart thuds as I thank her for coming to the show. I can't remember being this flustered in a long time.

Sophie's soft cheeks blush as she lets me know how much she enjoyed our concert. She tells me she loves my music—I can't help but recall the image of her at my show, singing along with me under the strobe lights. She's stolen a special place in this rocker's heart for sure.

Sophie had heard the news that my band got signed by a big time record company and congratulates me with an awkward hug before the bell rings. It gives me goose bumps. I want to follow her like a stray pup to her next class and talk about music. I want to stare into her beautiful, ocean-like eyes and find out her favorite color; her favorite food; if she has any brothers or sisters, but we only get to talk for two minutes—the best two minutes of my entire day.

Miss Heather is still trying to cling to me because of all the attention that Cellar Door Is Gone is getting. She loves it when the other students come up and ask me for autographs, but it's a very strange concept for me. I actually find it kind of ridiculous, but I always oblige. I have friends that I've gone to school with since kindergarten who are now asking for my signature. It's so weird.

Kyle pretends to be my assistant, and has the students form a line when needed, especially when hot girls are involved. I find myself putting my John Hancock on some really odd stuff—lunch tickets, a progress report, a volleyball, and you can't believe how many hands and arms.

My sis strolls up as I'm signing a group of students' geometry homework. Kyle is in full personal manager mode and asks her if she wants to butt into the front of the line.

Megan just shakes her head. "Puhleeeease—like I need his signature. I taught that little squirt how to write his name when he was still using crayons." She says with a coy attitude and big grin.

"Oh, so that's how it is?" Kyle laughs.

"Yup. That's how it is," Megan replies with a wink and continues down the hall, cool as a cucumber. If I didn't know better, I'd swear that my sister is flirting with my best friend.

I quickly and literally shake that idea out of my brain before it scars me for life.

D.J. and Sam strut by as several students linger. The two football jocks break through the crowd that has gathered. "Oh, Forrest, will you sign an autograph for us?" D.J. mocks in a swooning feminine tone. He holds his hand over his heart looking as though he might faint at any moment.

"Sure, come on over," I dare. The wheels in my head are turning. Sam and D.J. take me up on the dare. Trying to humiliate me, the two football jocks lift up their shirts. D.J. is proud to expose his tanning-bed-tanned six-pack abs. And then there's Sam. He exposes his pasty white stomach that's bulging like a keg.

"Put it right here," D.J. says smoothly, pointing to his chiseled mid-section.

"Be glad to," I agree, nonchalantly. I begin to

quickly scribble across their mid-sections with my permanent, black Sharpie pen. More students gather around the autograph session and begin to laugh and point as I finish up.

"What's so funny?" Sam asks dully, as he stands behind D.J. The volume of the laughter increases as D.J. and Sam turn to look at each other's supposed autographs. I watch a combination of fury and humiliation well up on their faces as they quickly pull their jerseys down and storm off to the boy's bathroom. I had written on each of them with bold, black, indelible marker: **I'M WITH STUPID** with a big arrow pointing straight up.

"Who's Stupid? I don't get it, D.J.," Sam mumbles. He's clueless.

Yes. Sweet revenge—a dish best served well-chilled!

Our school week wraps up and Saturday night rolls in. Our main man Frank scored the boys and me tickets for the hottest concert in town. I almost flip when he tells us who we are going to see. It's my all-time favorite band in the history of metal bands—the mighty Metallica!

I've actually been called mini-James Hetfield by disc jockeys. It's a thrill and honor since the Metallica front man has inspired me so greatly. We even share the same birthday—August third. He doesn't know it, but I consider him my soul rock-bro for sure.

Megan generously offers to drive the whole band to the B.O.K. Center for the concert. It's no secret that Jake, Randy and Cody love the way she harmlessly flirts with them. It's something that I can do without, but Megan is paying for the gas, and at $3.59 a gallon, I'll gratefully let her. I know that Mama won't let me drive solo in the city at night, so I have to put up with it for the evening.

As usual, Jake, Randy and Cody are running late again. Megan and I have to wait over fifteen minutes for them. I tell the boys that I'm sure they're gonna to be late for their own funerals. I can't help but be frustrated. I know the line for the concert is going to be huge.

I figured correctly. Megan drops the boys and me at the B.O.K Center and, just as I thought, the line winds more than half way around the immense arena. The crowd is heavy metal—just our style. Many of the concert goers recognize the boys and me. We take pictures with several fans and visit with Phil and Brent, the D.J.s from our local radio station, KMOD. They were the first D.J.s to play a Cellar Door Is Gone song on the air. We were just twelve years old.

The two brash comedians love to tease us about our age. In our last interview, they razzed me about the peach fuzz on my chin and asked me how in the world my voice could be so deep since I hadn't even hit puberty yet—good old Phil and Brent.

We wait outside the venue for over thirty minutes. Randy is hungry and complaining about the long line. He's going on and on about hot dogs and cheese pretzels when I hear my name being called out by a sweet voice. I lean around the snaking line and see a bright, shining, familiar face. It's Sophie!

"Forrrrrest!" she yells, as she makes her way down the disorderly line, eventually hugging each of us. "I knew you'd be here!" Sophie beams. She looks cuter than ever. "Hey, you guys. Follow me. I'll get you into the building."

We all follow closely as she leads our group with confidence. She looks so adorable in her black leggings, Metallica hoodie, and turquoise blue chucks. I love the way Sophie looks, but more than that I am in with love her positive personality and giving spirit. She's so bubbly and friendly. She's soooo different from Heather.

Sophie continues to lead us down a chrysanthemum-lined sidewalk that brings us to a side door of the slick, glass-paneled building. A guy that looks like he's in the Secret Service promptly opens the door as Sophie flashes the laminated pass that hangs on a neon pink Hello Kitty lariat around her neck.

"My dad works for the B.O.K. Center and gets the best tickets to the concerts and shows," she informs us, with a humble shrug of her shoulders.

"This is freakin' awesome! I can't believe we don't hav'ta stand out in that long line!" Jake exclaims.

"Where are your tickets?" Sophie asks, getting down to business.

"We're in the nosebleed section," I admit with disappointment.

"Not anymore," Sophie declares, as she plucks our tickets from our fingers one by one. She leads the boys and me down a dark ramp that opens up to the glorious floor-seating area.

Sophie directs us to our new, plush, upholstered seats just four rows back from the stage. I think I might actually hear a choir of angels singing as I realize just how close we're going to be to the stage.

"Is this okay?" she asks, with a sly smile on her pretty face.

"Is this okay? Is this *okay*? Yes, I do believe this is *very* okay!" I hug Sophie, lift her off her feet and swing her around. She lets out a giggle and a shriek, just like Mama always does when I'm being ornery and pick her up.

"Well, at least we don't have to pack a lunch for our trek up the stairs," Cody interjects dryly. I set Sophie back down and we connect with a perfect snapping high-five.

"Speaking of lunch, I'm gonna go get a hot dog, a pretzel, some popcorn and nachos with jalapeños and a Diet Coke...Y'all want anything?" Randy asks. We all laugh in unison at his concession stand grocery list.

Sophie fits in great with my bandmates—just like one of the guys. On the other hand, I can never in a million years imagine my band buds hanging out with Heather.

We all settle into our prime seats for the best concert of our lives. It's such a rush to be hanging out with someone of the opposite sex who likes the same music as me. Sophie is definitely a rad rocker chick.

I stand close by her side, sneaking glances at her perfect, angelic face. I notice her ears are gauged. They're awesome—just the right size with small, light catching, aquamarine stones that match the color of her eyes. I have gauges, too. My mom was cool. She let me get it done, but made it clear I wasn't to go over a double-zero. She understood I wanted an edgy look, but also knew I might get tired of having holes in my head someday. The size I gauged to could still close up if I left them out over time. One of Mama's favorite quotes is from Thomas Jefferson: "In matters of style, swim with the current; in matters of principle, stand like a rock." She has this quote hung up in my music room. I know exactly what it means.

The concert is beyond amazing. Sophie's perfectly neat hairstyle gets mussed as she flings her head to the rhythm of the heavy metal songs. I love the way her cheeks flush as she rocks out. I find myself loving everything about Sophie. She doesn't put on airs. What you see was what you get with her—I sure like what I see.

Just when I think the night can't get any better, it does. As Metallica is finishing its encore song, James Hetfield looks my way. Holding up his guitar pick, the mega-rocker motions toward me. He launches the pic in the air. I reach up above the surging crowd and stretch open my fingers. To my utter amazement, I catch the tiny, treasured piece of silver-flecked plastic. I open my hand slowly, showing Sophie I've secured it.

"The pic of destiny!" Sophie screams with excitement. She puts her soft hands over mine. Her midnight blue fingernail polish sparkles under the stage lights.

I'm dumbstruck. "Thank you for one of the best nights of my entire life!" I yell to her over the roaring cheers of the rocking crowd.

"You're totally welcome, Forrest. This is definitely the best concert I've ever been to—besides yours of course!" Sophie returns sincerely. She smiles back at me with a slight hint of shyness.

Sophie and I stand hip to hip, the crowd of thousands surrounding us seems to disappear. I recall the silly comment Randy had made about Megan and her perfume.

I understand now why he had that goof-ball look on his face. Sophie smells like sweet vanilla and fresh oranges. I stand next to her with a starry-eyed expression, inhaling the intoxicating scent that is Sophie. There's nowhere else in the world I would rather be at this moment—I am officially crushin'.

As my band buds and I give our heroes, the mighty Metallica, one last standing ovation, I realize that I'm totally and completely falling for this cool, rocker-chick, marching band, amazing girl named Sophie.

CHAPTER TWELVE

Another boring Monday morning at school rolls around, and is creeping by as Mondays at school tend to do. I sit in history class doodling on my Civil War quiz and daydreaming about Sophie and the incredible Metallica concert. I reach in my pocket and pull out the "pic of destiny," as Sophie had named it. I've officially made it my new good luck charm.

As I continue to draw little swirls and stars and zone out, I feel my cell phone vibrate. It's cruel and unusual torture for the teachers to allow us to have our cell phones on us, all the while knowing if we're caught using them during class time, they're taken away. It's like giving a five-year old a candy bar, and telling him to put it in his pocket until lunchtime—virtually impossible.

I know easygoing Mrs. Smith won't confiscate my phone, so I retrieve my BlackBerry from my hoodie pocket, hold it under my desktop and click on the message screen. It's a text from Mama.

Hey, Forrest! U r never going to believe where u boys are gonna be playin nxt Sunday... :)

She leaves me hanging in suspense until I retrieve the second message.

THE DALLAS COWBOYS!! Half-time at Texas Stadium!!! :0 Woo-Hoo!

I suddenly get dizzy with excitement. With shaking hands, I text Jake, Randy and Cody, who are sitting in the classroom with me just five rows back. The four of us race to Mrs. Smith's desk and request hall passes in unison.

Mrs. Smith is so flustered she drops her hall pass pad and crafty, silk daisy-topped ink pen. We're flipping out and ready to celebrate the news. One by one, she writes out the passes. One by one, we spill out into the silent, empty hallway where Jake, Randy, Cody, and I begin doing an impromptu victory dance. We high-five each other and attempt to scream in raspy whispers. Two girls on their way to the office with attendance sheets see us jigging around and whisper-screaming. I'm pretty sure they think we've lost our ever-loving minds.

We do our best rendition of Jed Clampet's *Beverly Hillbillies* hoe down. Cody grabs one of the leery co-eds and spins her around twice as though they're at a local VFW square dance. The bell rings. The boys and I collect ourselves into one tight group hug before we float our way back into Mrs. Smith's classroom to pick up our textbooks.

The rest of the school day seems to crawl along, but finally the last hour arrives. I can't wait to share the news with my football team and the coaches, and when I do, they're all so stoked for me. Except for D.J., that is. My football buds request an 8 x 10 glossy of the Dallas Cowboys Cheerleaders for the locker room, and Coach Bryan is completely blown away by the fact that I'll be standing on the same field with the Dallas Cowboys and Baltimore Ravens. I revel in the sweet moment while D.J sulks by himself in the weight room doing bicep work. Coweta's team jerseys are orange and black, but it's clear D.J.'s only color is envy-green today.

After football practice, I head to Aunt Carmen's for band practice. I motor down the dusty dirt road with my radio cranked and flip through my iPod to find a Taylor Swift song that I've strategically hidden among my heavy rock tunes and metal music. Listening to Taylor Swift is one of my guilty pleasures. Taylor's popular tune "You Belong With Me" blares as I belt out the chorus. There's no one here to make fun of me. Only the generic, black and white Holstein cows chewing their cud lazily in the field are witnesses to my complete insanity. I think of Sophie as I sing along—the words remind me so much of her. I wonder if she has Taylor's album. I'm sure she does. I wonder if she thinks of me when she sings along with the song. I hope she does.

When I arrive home, Dad meets me at the door.

He wears a strange, controlled grin. "Bud, I'm beginning to think your rock-n-roll dream is starting to pay off. Your mom and I both are going to go with you to the Dallas game on Sunday."

Are my ears deceiving me? Is my dad actually congratulating me on my band's success? Mama just laughs and asks Dad if his excitement has anything to do with getting to see the Dallas Cowboys Cheerleaders up close and personal.

Dad smiles and says, "Maybe."

The day of the NFL game arrives with great anticipation. Our families are totally floored by the accommodations for us at Texas Stadium. We're personally escorted to a green room. It isn't even painted green, but is a term for the special waiting room reserved for V.I.P.s, or "very important persons." It's stocked with all the food and beverages we could ever want to consume.

Cody drinks five Red Bulls and is bouncing off the walls. Randy's in finger food heaven. My parents and Megan are thoroughly enjoying being exposed to "the good life." Jake and I explore the Sky Box that's reserved for us. It looks like a fancy living room, complete with an overstuffed, off-white couch, big screen TV and glass coffee tables. Our families are going to get to watch the game here in luxurious comfort. Servers in crisp white shirts glide in and out, refilling trays ruffled with fancy green lettuce. We feel like rock-n-roll royalty as our parents toast us with a glass of complimentary bubbly.

Just before the game begins, Mama

announces that she's going to go down onto the field to take pictures of us during the half time show. She's so very sentimental and loves taking photographs. Mama always has at least two electronic devices on hand at all times to capture special moments. Her reserve includes two camcorders, a flip cam, three digital cameras, a cell phone camera, an old Nikon 35 mm camera, plus a big bag of back up batteries and chargers for them all. Megan and I have nicknamed her "Mama-razzi." She gets lots of, "Oh, Mom, that's enough pictures," from Megan and me, but our scrapbooks are fat with happy memories that we'll cherish in the years to come.

Our band is in place and set to play two Cellar Door Is Gone songs for the Dallas half time show. The Dallas Cowboys Cheerleaders have even choreographed a dance to our new single, "Rocket." The boys and I are so stoked. We aren't as nervous as we thought we'd be, playing in front of sixty-five thousand football fans, because we get to lip-sync the songs. My vocals will be covered up by the professionally recorded track. We can all just chill and jam out.

Frank has a quick pep talk with us in the end zone. He makes an off-color remark about the Dallas Cowboys Cheerleaders provocative uniforms, and then sends us on our way with a "Do work soldiers!"

Jake, Randy, Cody, and I jump on the mobile stage. We're mesmerized by the crowd. The diehard football fans look like tiny, fidgeting insects in the stands of the gigantic stadium. I inhale deeply and take in the view from the thirty-yard line. It's absolutely breathtaking. I feel like I'm king of the world. Goose bumps rise on my forearms as my brain buzzes into killer rock mode.

I shake my shoulders and jump up and down in place like a prizefighter a few times to loosen up. I realize I have a white-knuckle death grip on my guitar. One by one, I stretch and contract my fingers and now I'm ready for action. Camera lights glare, amps sputter, and producers run around frantically with headsets and walkie-talkies. There's a frenzy of activity, and then half time begins.

The stage is immediately rushed by a predetermined group of teens who proceed to rock out with us. It's craziness! The boys and I are really killin' it, or so we think. We strike the last note of the last song and as the gorgeous Dallas Cowboys Cheerleaders begin their synchronized exit from the field, thousands of football fans break out into raucous boos. I even hear the stinging phrase, "you suck," being slung with audacity from the packed stands.

My heart begins to thud and my blood pressure climbs. I know my face is turning at least three shades of red. The boys and I practically sprint from the mobile stage and gather by the large archway that separates the field from the underbelly of the stadium. We feel so insignificant as we stand dumbfounded and numb. We watch the herd of massive NFL football players charge back onto the field for the second half.

"Man, they hated us! Did you hear them booing?" Jake asks, bewildered.

"Dude, I thought they were rockin' out," Cody says quietly. He has the same forlorn look on his face that my cocker spaniel, Stella, had when she got scolded for chewing up one of Dad's comfy O.U. Sooner house slippers.

Randy and I are just flat out speechless. We turn to make our way back to the "Dallas blue" green room. I dread the inevitable bad review we're about to receive from Frank. The boys and I walk slowly, kicking at the turf when, to our surprise, the entire Dallas Cowboys cheerleading squad in all their blue and white glory comes running our way. This traffic-stopping group of hotties is shaking its glittering, silver pom-poms and prancing in a beeline straight for us. The cheerleaders take turns high fiving and congratulating us.

The cheerleaders' coach is the last in line to hug our necks. She's all smiles and bubbly. It takes our minds off our busted performance for a moment. My buds and I are in awe but still really confused.

"Hey, Coach Keli...were we that bad?" I ask. I don't really want to hear the answer. My face is still burning crimson red with embarrassment.

"What, honey? Noooo. You boys were fantastic! Your songs were great! We loved it!" Coach Keli insists.

"Then why was the crowd booing us so loudly?" I ask, still puzzled and numb.

"Oh my goodness, boys. They weren't booing *you*. The Dallas fans were booing the Ravens' team coming back onto the field. They were booing their rivals!" Coach Keli laughs and grabs me. The pit in my stomach begins to ease. She gives me a sweet motherly hug. Our embarrassment fades away with her words. "They loved you!" Keli assures.

Sweet relief floods over us all as we watch the cheerleaders strut their stuff down the cement walkway that leads to their locker room. Cody somehow gets caught smack dab in the middle of the group of beautiful women. His purple and red Mohawk is a static mess and zipping out in all directions as though someone rubbed his head with a balloon. The girls vigorously shake their pom-poms all around him.

"Grab my camera, dude! Pleeeease get a pic of this!" Cody begs, as he's swept away by the mass of cheerleaders. The huge, goofy grin is the biggest I've ever seen on Cody's normally stoic face.

Jake, Randy and I bolt like lightening to catch up in hopes that the bevy of shapely babes in white stretchy hot pants will kidnap us as well. "Mama-razzi" multi-tasks as she snaps pictures with one hand and camcords with the other. She yells for us to us to look her way. Needless to say, we can't hear a single word she's saying—our focus is elsewhere!

CHAPTER THIRTEEN

It's two weeks since my band and I performed at the Dallas Cowboys' half-time show, and another exciting opportunity is apparently sailing our way. Frank called in on speakerphone with some incredible news: the boys and I will be heading to the Big Apple on Tuesday to play a showcase at MTV for bigwigs in the music industry! We feel like we're on a wild, winding head rush of a rollercoaster ride with season tickets to the amusement park.

Jake, Randy and Cody are stoked that we'll have to miss a couple more days of school. I, on the other hand, really do like school and have mixed feelings about missing my classes. I'm the black sheep of the rock-and-roll flock. In stark contrast to the rocker image, I have a 4.0 average, and usually try to hide the fact that I'm in the National Honor Society for students. I enjoy socializing with my friends and, of course, I love playing high school football.

Now that I've got my eye on a cutie in the marching band, I find myself liking school even more. I build my days around seeing Sophie in the halls between classes. Just a glimpse of her friendly face can put me in a good mood for the entire afternoon.

Heather, however, has worn my nerves paper thin. I continue trying to find the right opportunity to break up with her. I've been so consumed with the band and the whirlwind we're in, I just can't face the drama that I know will ensue. Heather is in groupie girl heaven. She isn't about to be pushed out of the spotlight, either. She flirts with all the football players...heck, all the wrestlers and the entire baseball team as well, but is agitated if I even say hello to any female, especially Sophie. Heather ignores no opportunity to intentionally belittle her in front of me.

Today is no different. I cringe when I hear Heather's voice coming from behind us, as Sophie and I stand making small talk about my trip to New York City. *Here it comes.* I know Sophie's in for public humiliation.

"Oh, Sweeeeetie," Heather says, so anyone yards away can hear as she sidles up to me coolly. "You *must* be lost. The *band* room is that way, dear!" She points and steps between Sophie and me.

Heather gives me a peck on the cheek, leaving a greasy, bubble gum-scented lip gloss imprint on my face that I immediately wipe off with the back of my hand.

"Now, Forrest, be sure to call me the minute you get to New York," Heather orders, "and bring me back a t-shirt, too, sweetie pie," she continues, with a southern bell tone. Her words are coated with the same artificial sweetener that coats her intention.

By the look in Sophie's eyes I can tell she feels inferior to Heather. She lowers her eyes and walks away. I want to run after her, but Heather grabs my arm.

"In a small size, okay?" she continues, as she bats her long, mascara-coated eyelashes at me. I used to see the future in her emerald green eyes, but now they just seem as cold as a snake to me.

"Whatever, Heather...sure," I return as I wipe my cheek one more time to remove the final residue of her superficial kiss. I look to the end of the hall as Sophie looks back at me. Just before she disappears around the corner, she gives me an innocent glance, shrugs her shoulders and lifts her hand in a comforting gesture. It's almost as if she feels sorry for me. She's such a sweetheart who doesn't deserve to be treated rudely by anyone, especially Heather.

At football practice this afternoon, I have a heart-to-heart talk with Coach Bryan. I have to let him know that I'll be missing two days of practice. I promise to double-time my workouts when I return to make up for my absence. Coach knows I'm good for it, and says that he has a feeling he's about to lose a linebacker to the cause of rock-n-roll.

The next morning, I can hardly pry my eyes open and roll out of bed. Mama and I are awake at 4:30 a.m. in order to be at the Tulsa airport by 6:00. I always pictured the life of a rock star as staying up playing all night and sleeping till noon every day. That was not the case.

"These are not rocker-friendly hours, dude...I'm a musician, not a paperboy," I wine, yawning weakly. Mama and I drive through the nearly deserted streets. She agrees, and returns the contagious, open-mouthed oxygen intake as we make a stop at Quick Trip to pick up Red Bull roadies. Last week I tried to drink a cup of Dad's black coffee for a pick-me-up, but it tasted like hot liquid mud. Thank the Lord for Red Bull.

Our flight is uneventful. We have an hour layover in Chicago. We eat deep-dish pizza at the airport, and then fly on into the big city. The boys, our families and I are met outside the terminal by a polite gentleman dressed in khakis and a blue, button-down shirt, who ushers us into a white, unmarked passenger van. This was the exact vehicle that Mama always told me to be leery of when I was younger. She calls them "Lester the molester" vans.

As we near the downtown area of New York City, I can see it's like a whole new world. I feel like a clueless, country mouse—a little town hick in a massive, bustling city. The boys and I are in total awe of the zipping, yellow taxi cabs and droves of pedestrians that plough their way down the crowded city streets. I can't help but wonder how many people have been waylaid by the unforgiving taxis as they honk impatiently and graze the hips of stragglers, yakking on their cell phones, in the busy intersections.

I start feeling surprisingly intoxicated by the city's metropolitan buzz, and its vibrant rhythm. It's so different from my serene, slow-paced, red dirt town back in Oklahoma.

Our group bounds out of the van into a bleak parking lot and we make our way down the east side of the towering Waldorf Hotel. I round the corner and am blitzed by the neon lights of Times Square. I've seen it on TV. Every year we watch Dick Clark's New Year's Eve countdown to watch the ball drop, but seeing it live and in person is unbelievable.

I can't believe my eyes. It's like looking through a giant, constantly changing kaleidoscope. The brilliant colors and lights flash and move in precise order, hurling advertisements in my face. I think about Dad's obsession of turning lights off at our house and wonder just how outrageous New York City's electric bill must be each month.

Jake, Randy, Cody, and I are herded by our protective chaperones. We cautiously and curiously wander down Broadway. As we look down the street, there, standing in the center median, is a buff, very tan man playing his acoustic guitar in nothing but a straw cowboy hat, cowboy boots and tighty-whities! Our guide tells us he's known as "The Naked Cowboy."

I spot tourists trading dollar bills for a picture with the guitar wrangler. Of course, Mama has to capture this on film. I quickly snatch the camera from Mama and motion for her to pose with the under-dressed musician.

"Blaaackmaaail!" I sing out as the flash blinks. Mama giggles as the Naked Cowboy gives her a big squeeze and collects her crumpled dollar bill.

"Man, if I would've known that this was all it took to make money out here, I would've thrown my jeans out of the van window." Cody says, barely audible over the honking cabbies.

"Yeah, and I would've brought Coach Bryan's cowboy hat, dude!" I chime in.

If the Naked Cowboy had been standing on a corner in Coweta, it wouldn't be a tourist attraction. We'd just assume he had too much to drink the night before and forgot where he parked his truck. In our first thirty minutes in New York, we already have a great story to take back home—and pics to prove it.

We have an hour and a half before we need to be in the MTV studio, so we all decide to do a little sightseeing. Our group crosses the jammed street on a wing and a prayer, and is confronted by the biggest Toys R Us store that any of us have ever seen. We have to check it out.

Mama and the other parents relish the fact that of all the exciting places to go in the city—The Empire State Building, The Statue of Liberty, etc.—Jake, Randy, Cody, and I want to go to a toy store. We're still their little boys at heart.

But this fantasy store isn't your typical mall shopping experience. It's several stories high and accommodates an incredible, fully operational Ferris wheel that's built right smack dab in the middle of the store.

Being a major superhero fan, the first thing that catches my eye as I enter the mega-store is Spider-Man in the flesh. Today I'm sporting my black, flat-bill Batman cap. I'm not sure if they're on the same team, but I'm itching to get a pic with Spidey, anyway.

I approach the skulking superhero dressed in his iconic, blue and red stretchy suit. I nod and ask if I can get a picture with him. A store employee steps in and explains that she would have to take the picture, after which I'd have to purchase it at a store kiosk for ten dollars.

I decide against it—Mama and I are on a tight budget since it's house payment week back home. Smiling, I hold out my hand to Spiderman as a friendly gesture. To my surprise, the masked man begins to speak. His high pitched and slightly nerdy voice is somewhat muffled by the vented lycra covering his mouth, and totally throws me off guard.

"*Dude*...I know you! You're Forrest from Cellar Door Is Gone! I play your song 'Rocket' on *Rock*

Band all the time!" I can't believe he actually knows of me or my music. Several of our songs have been placed in the game *Rock Band*, which lets video gamers step into the rock-and-roll lifestyle. They can sing, drum and play guitar along with their favorite bands.

Apparently, Spider-Man, whose real name is Carl, is a *Rock Band* fanatic!

"Hey, man. Let your mom take all the pics she wants," Spidey Carl gushes, as he begins to pose with me. The pictures will be great. Spider-Man and I strike our most brutal rock stance and flash the rock sign together. A framed, three-by-five photo will definitely be placed next to my Superman alarm clock at home.

After the boys and I run wild in the toy store for almost an hour, shooting Nerf hoops and trying out the newest *Gears of War* X-Box video game, we're ushered back together. Acting like ten year olds was fun, but now it's time to rock. We cautiously step back into the street jam packed with the bustling pedestrians, and make our way back to the MTV studio.

The *TRL* staging room is filled with hipsters from the music and entertainment industry. I was raised on MTV music videos, and to be standing in the middle of their studio is totally surreal. Jake, Randy, Cody, and I feed off the catchy modern energy of the big city. Our four song set is in-your-face raw and exciting.

Cameras flash as the ultra-hip music execs bob

their heads. A journalist from the *New York Post* takes notes, with a look of delighted disbelief on his face. The boys and I give another killer performance. We rock the MTV studio.

Frank rubs elbows with the P.R. officials and works on making connections for the band. My job, as front man, is to keep shaking hands. One official looking gentleman tells me that I had better put on my Ray Bans, because the future looks very bright. I do my best to hold my composure and a perma-smile for the next thirty minutes. I don't want to seem like a country bumpkin. I try to act casual and relaxed like, "Yeah, I do this every day." I manage to keep my cool on the outside, but inside I'm ready to jump out of my skin with excitement.

After the meet-and-greet, Jake, Randy, Cody, and I make our way back to the green room—this one is painted cherry red and has funky gold molding—for a catered lunch of authentic New York deli pastrami sandwiches, fruit and the best cheesecake any of us has ever eaten. Randy has two strawberry-drizzled pieces and gets a stomach ache.

The boys and I check out some of the photos hanging in the MTV hallways. We are thrilled to see how many famous musicians have played this same *TRL* stage. Justin Timberlake is a particular favorite of mine.

I feel like I have to pinch myself to make sure I'm not just dreaming. Actually Jake does pinch me to make sure it's all real.

"Ouch!" I flinch, rubbing the sting out of my arm.

"Yep…it's real!" Jake confirms.

Our band is graciously allowed to loot the MTV store, courtesy of the channel's vice-president. Each of us leaves with three huge bags of swag—which is a fancy word for free stuff— ranging from clocks to hoodies, and t-shirts and pillows embossed with the MTV logo. Cody and I elbow each other. We wonder how in the world we're going to get our treasures back, considering we can only have one carry-on bag individually, and our cheap suitcases are the size of a bread box.

We wander back down Broadway, smiling widely at strangers, dodging taxi cabs and gawking at the big city lights. Our well-worn chucks are sticking to the dirty New York City sidewalks, but our heads are in the clouds. All four of us boys are in MTV heaven.

CHAPTER FOURTEEN

Jake, Randy, Cody and I gather around the bales of hay that make up the seating at the jam barn. The trip to New York City had been so thrilling that it lit a fire under us and now we're practicing harder than ever.

Our manager enters the practice barn with the look of an important announcement on his face, which peaks our curiosity. We're told to gather our families and wait for him there.

Frank drags open the old barn door and shakes his head as he surveys our families, seated on the bales of musty, pale yellow straw. Mojo nickers from his stall as three barn cats dart under Frank's Italian leather loafers, nearly tripping him. He laughs with frustration and says that there is no way he could ever explain to others in the industry just how "down home" this situation is. They would have to see it to believe it.

"Bales of hay for chairs...really? Wild cats running everywhere...seriously? Mr. Ed as a mascot...Judas Priest!" Frank grumbles as he tries to regain his balance. Bits of straw and fur fly in the dusty air as the fraidy cats vacate the premises. He sneezes twice, clears his throat, coughs and tells us in a nasally tone, "Oh, fantastic, I think I'm allergic to hay and cats!" He coughs a few more times.

Our manager finally composes himself, and takes a long draw from his emerald green bottle of Pellegrino sparkling water. Eventually, he begins to speak with great enthusiasm.

"Okay, rock stars...you cats were a mega hit in The Big Apple. I'm stoked to tell you boys that your single, "Rocket," is getting heavy radio play. It's made it to the top fifteen on the active rock charts. We think it just might be a bullet! I wanted to gather you boys and your parental units together today to tell you about our next trip."

Frank clears his throat dramatically one last time and pauses for what seems like an eternity. "Believe it or not, my young dudes, we are traveling to Stockholm, Sweden...to open for the one and only legends of rock, KISS!" He exhales and begins to clap.

There is a collective gasp in the barn and then looks of shock and disbelief all around. KISS is one of my band's rock heroes. Several of our moms and dads had seen KISS in concert back in the day, and they are as thrilled as we are.

The boys and I bound from our seats and snazzy-dressing Frank becomes a victim of a Cellar Door Is Gone takedown. We throw our arms around our manager and give him our classic, extreme group hug, which knocks us all backward over a hay bale.

Frank gets back onto his feet and begins picking straw from his brand new Ed Hardy t-shirt imprinted with a ferocious, fang bearing tiger. "Congrats, young rockers! We'll be leaving a week from Thursday. You rock stars will have to miss a couple of days of school, so let your teachers know." This news brings even bigger smiles to Jake, Randy and Cody's faces.

"An MTV camera crew will be coming along to film the whole trip. You can each bring one parent as your chaperone, so let me know who's going and we'll shoot the passport info through on the fast track. We'll get the airline tickets, as well. All right—this is how we roll, baby!" Frank spouts as he shoots index finger pistols at us.

My celebration experiences a hiccup when I suddenly remember that if my football team wins their game this Friday, we'll be vying for the State Championship. My elation turns to confusion, and when my eyes connect with Dad's, I know he's thinking the same thing. Dad sits quietly, nervously tapping his fingers on his Levis. He has a blank look of apathy on his face. I suck a deep breath of oxygen in and replay the words in my head that Mama always tells me when I am worried. She says,

"Just remember the old song, 'One Day at a Time, Sweet Jesus,' and change it to 'one hour at a time'—anything can be managed that way." So I guess hour to hour, Sweet Jesus it is.

The next morning at school, the news of my band's trip to Sweden to open for KISS is already spreading like wildfire. It's another head-spinning day. I feel like I'm in a bubble floating as a spectator away from reality. There have been so many changes.

I haven't been spending much time with Heather. She's started driving herself into school for the past couple of weeks. I've started going in thirty minutes early to put in extra time on my geometry. We still eat lunch together most days with mutual friends, and meet at our lockers after sixth hour. Each and every time I try to talk to Heather about a break up, she just won't have it. She pouts. Her green eyes become liquid with tears and she says how much she likes me. Even though I don't believe her sincerity, I'm soft-hearted, and am not ready to go to drama city. I decide to put the confrontation off until next week. I'll make the break official after Sweden for sure.

In the meantime, I can't get the image of Sophie, her blonde hair, blue eyes and room-lighting smile, off my mind.

CHAPTER FIFTEEN

I hope I see Sophie today on my way to the field house sixth hour. She's the band director's aid. Sometimes I catch a glimpse of her through the small rectangular window in Mr. Brandt's band room door as I pass by on my way to football.

Today I'm feeling brave. I peek in the door and see Sophie sitting at the piano. She's playing a soft, hypnotic melody. I stand for just a moment getting lost in the piece with her. I sure don't want to appear to be a creeper, so I crack the creaky band room door open further. She is all alone.

"Hey, Forrest!" Sophie senses the door opening, stops playing and greets me cheerfully. I grin widely as I enter, casually surveying the room. It's filled with shiny brass instruments, bongos, drums, xylophones, bells, and black, mottled music stands.

She smiles back and gushes enthusiastically, "I heard about your trip to Sweden. *Wow, Forrest*!! You're opening for KISS!"

Her friendly face is all lit up. "I also heard "Rocket" on the radio this morning. The song is soooo catchy! It's really great. I know you've got to be beyond excited," she adds.

I'm listening to her voice, but find myself distracted by the fragrance of her orangey-vanilla perfume.

"Oh...oh, man, you know it! I can't believe how things are takin' off for us. It's just kinda freakin' me out. Sometimes I don't know whether I'm comin' or goin'," I reply. "How've you been, Sophie?"

I can't believe it, but my palms are actually sweating. I can play in front of hundreds—shoot, *thousands*—of people and keep my cool, but put me alone in a room with Sophie and I begin to sweat, stutter and generally just fall all over myself.

"I've been good," Sophie says with downcast eyes, making me feel as though this isn't exactly the truth. "I hope you don't think I'm stuck up when I don't speak to you in the halls sometimes. It's just...Heather's usually around and I don't think she likes me much. You two make a really cute couple...she's so pretty." Sophie replies with a bit of hesitation.

I'm certain that Heather would add Sophie's compliment to her "daily list" if she had heard it.

"No way Sophie...I know you better than that. Yeah, Heather's pretty and popular...but I don't know," I stammer. She's just not very *nice*," I blurt out. "I've been trying to break up with her—for sure gonna call it quits after I get back from Sweden."

As I explain in muttering fashion, an acoustic guitar sitting in the corner of the band room catches my eye. I had actually been working on a song that I've written with Sophie as my inspiration. I started writing it the night after the Metallica concert.

"I just can't thank you enough for the amazing seats you got us at the concert. You mind?" I ask, as I cross to pick up the glossy black Ibanez resting in a guitar stand.

"Be my guest," Sophie says, not knowing exactly what to expect.

I can see that she's picked up a pair of nicked drumsticks from the top of the piano and begins fidgeting with them.

Could she be nervous, too? I wonder to myself. I try to keep my cool. "This is a song I've been working on. It's really different from what I usually play," I explain as I strum the first chords. *Do* not *sing off key*, I mentally order myself as I begin the song.

There's a girl in my eyes
And she's lookin' my way
I feel so close to her on a windy day
This girl I've fallen for is a light in my dark world
Her smile carries me away
Her smile carries me awaaay

I sing from my heart as I continue the soft, heartfelt ballad that I've secretly named "Sophie's Song." I can see Sophie blush slightly as I finish the last line in my song. I strum the last note, letting it ring out invisibly and soft as it dissolves in the air. Ending with a sheepish grin, I glance in her direction.

Sophie is smiling, too. I can spot that hopeful smile of hers from twenty lockers away in the hall. It always makes my heart beat a little faster.

I stroll back across the room and replace the guitar gingerly in the stand. I suddenly become very self-conscious. I hope I look cool in my skinny jeans and Pac Sun tee. I really hope Sophie liked the song.

"Forrest...oh my gosh! That was *amazing*!" Sophie exclaims. "You should definitely record that one!" she says earnestly. Her eyes are clear and truthful.

Whew...she liked it! I think with relief. *Gosh, her eyes are so beautiful!*

"I'll pray for you guys to have a safe trip." Sophie continues thoughtfully.

The more time I spend with Sophie, the more I can see the beauty inside her heart. She's truly a special girl—one-of-a-kind for sure.

"Thanks, Sopie." I return. "I'm glad you liked it. Well, I'd better get to football. I dread the thought of talkin' to Coach. If we win on Friday, we're gonna be in the State Championship game, and I'll be halfway across the world in Sweden.," I reply quietly. "I've been really confused lately...a lot of decisions to make."

It's all a little overwhelming—knowing that I'd have to disappoint Heather, no matter how snide she's been, by choosing Sophie, but most of all my dad by choosing my music over football.

"Just follow your heart, Forrest. It'll all be okay," Sophie says quietly in a comforting tone.

It's so refreshing that her words are totally sincere, and are about me, not her. That's something I never get from Heather. Just follow my heart...I think my heart has just officially chosen Sophie.

"Good luck at your football game. I'll be rooting you guys on," Sophie adds, clasping her hands together just like Mama does when she gives me words of encouragement. I decide, on the spur of the moment, to lean in and give Sophie a quick hug goodbye. She feels so little in my arms. She feels like the one little thing I'm missing in my life.

I'm walking on air as I make my way to the field house. I notice three tiny, darting sparrows on the sidewalk pecking at a handful of discarded neon-orange Cheetos. I hear the afternoon breeze rattling the leaves of the cottonwoods. Everything just seems brighter and more real. I look up at the sky. I feel as though I'm moving right along with the ethereal clouds above, and all I'm thinking is, *Her smile really does carry me away!*

CHAPTER SIXTEEN

We're victorious—we win our football game tonight. My brain was not in the game, and I don't know what's wrong with me. I missed several important tackles, but thanks to our lightning-fast safety saving the day, my mistakes were not game-changers. My team is chugging like a freight train that can't be stopped, but I feel like I'm just a passenger along for the ride. The Coweta Tigers will be playing for the State Championship. My team, and the entire town, is ecstatic—but I feel indifferent.

My head swims in confusion. This is the big game I've dreamed of playing from the first time I set my cleats on the field for little league, and I'm going to miss it. I can't believe it. I don't want to let my teammates down, but I just can't pass up the opportunity of a lifetime with my band in Sweden. Luckily, the Tigers' lineup is deep. There are strong backup players waiting in the ranks.

The hardest part is dealing with my dad's disappointment. He's been giving me the silent treatment. The quieter my dad is, the more upset he is. After the game, Dad just gives me a firm look, a pat on the shoulder pad, and walks away. It's breaking my heart. I'm so torn. I can't remember a time when Dad and I were on the outs.

The following day, I still participate in football practice. As the final whistle blows, I jog off the field and head for the showers. I pause at the sight of the sun setting over the west bleachers. The sunset is blazing orange and purple. The oak trees in the distance look like they're sketched in black ink across the canvas of the evening sky.

I love sunrises and sunsets; they always inspire me. I stand gazing up as the fiery globe appears to be igniting the metallic bleachers and decide that my next song will have a sunset in it. My band and I will be leaving for Sweden tomorrow.

It suddenly hits me that this might be the last sunset I'll see from the fifty-yard line. I feel lonely and sad.

Inside the locker room, Coach's favorite Toby Keith song, "Made in America," is blaring on a dusty, circa 1990's boom box. The twangy, boot-scootin' tune elevates my mood. I hear Coach Bryan yell my name over the music.

"Hey, Forrest...ya ever think a cuttin' a country album?" Coach Bryan asks. His hick accent lays thick as biscuit gravy on his words. He spits a black, liquid stream of chewing tobacco juice into an empty Gatorade bottle.

"If I do, Coach, you will *definitely* be my inspiration!" I holler back, shaking my head.

"Ahhh, son, ya know, country music's where it's at," Coach says with absolute conviction. Coach crosses the room and places his well-worn black felt cowboy hat on my head. He pats me firmly on the back with his huge, callused hands. Coach is like a bear that doesn't know its own strength.

I squint my eyes shut and jolt forward a step, which prompts me to begin riding a fake bucking horse all the way to my locker. I swing an imaginary rope over my head, grab my Joe's Tire Shop ball cap and throw Coach back his cowboy hat like a Frisbee.

"It fits me pretty good, Coach, but I'd better let you keep it. You'll need it after the big game Friday. I'm not sure if the Swedes are ready for a cowboy from Coweta just yet!" I laugh.

"Hey, Forrest. Ya know we're all really proud a ya, bud. Knock em' dead, son! We're gonna miss ya on the field, but we're glad yer followin' yer dreams," Coach Bryan says, with genuine sincerity.

"Thanks, Coach. I can't tell you how much I appreciate all you've done for me." I feel my heart grow heavy.

"I know yer gonna see a lot more of this big ole world, Forrest," Coach returns. His smile widens in approval, revealing bits of brown tobacco in his teeth. "I just wish you would've learnt to play country music." He teases, as he slaps me on the back again. This time I brace myself and stand firm. I extend my hand and Coach shakes it firmly. The calluses on my hands from playing guitar are small compared to the calluses on Coach Bryan's hands, which developed from years of daily farm labor. I respect Coach more than I can say.

"KISS, huh? Well they ain't no Toby Keith, but I guess they'll do, son!"

On my way out of the locker room, I can hear the shrill sound of hair clippers buzzing. The trainer wielding shears turns to me as he shaves a no-neck lineman's hair down to a faint shadow of stubble.

"Hey, Forrest, come have a seat. I'll give ya a buzz cut!" he says, patting the back of the rusty metal folding chair.

"Oh, no thanks, dude. I'm good. Maybe I'll catch ya' when I get back." I kindly decline, as I shake my long, shaggy hair and replace my ball cap.

As I leave the locker room, I raise my hands over my head and jump up to smack the "Tiger Pride" sign that hangs above the heavy metal door. The sharp, cold evening air hits me square in the face. I inhale deeply. I turn back towards the dark, abandoned football field and yell at the top of my lungs, "GO TIGERS!!!" My voice echoes back in agreement twice, and then dies in the lonely black shadows.

CHAPTER SEVENTEEN

I arrive back home to a packing frenzy. Mama's bluesy Eric Clapton CD mingles with the mechanical sloshing sound of the washing machine's agitator. She has on her favorite old-as-the-hills Lynyrd Skynyrd t-shirt, and just as aged, faded, holey jeans. A glass of amber wine sparkles on the kitchen counter under the chandelier light.

"Wine...all right!" I tease. I raise the crystal glass to my lips and pretend to partake.

"Yeah, right." Mama huffs with an exhausted sigh. She takes the glass from my hand, swirls the liquid contents, takes a sip and then continues in her zone. Mama runs between the dryer, the ironing board and the suitcases as she gathers things for my trip to Sweden. As much as Mama wants to go, Dad will be the one who travels with me. I'm sure the glass of wine Mama has is intended to numb her disappointment.

The other boys are bringing their fathers as well, except for Jake. He'll be chaperoned by his favorite uncle. It's going to be a guy's trip. I wish Mama could go with us, too. I hug her tight and tell her she'll be my date if I ever get to go to The Grammys. I'm hoping the adventure will help take Dad's mind off of the football game. I hope it'll help take my mind off it, as well.

Mama's blonde braid snakes over her shoulder. She looks like a mad scientist as she measures out three-ounce bottles of shampoo, conditioner and, most importantly, my hair gel. We can only take three-ounce size liquids on the plane because of airline regulations, and I need extra gel because of my thick hair. Mama prides herself on finding the products that are just right for keeping my curls in check.

She laughs when she notices that she's packing more accessories for me than she would have packed for herself. Laid out on my bed are: four wrist bands (ranging from black leather, to metal, to terry cloth), three necklaces, two wallet chains, two leather silver-studded belts with heavy duty buckles, and last but not least, a blue and white knit scarf. I have to promise Mama that I'll wear it to keep the cold air from giving me a frog in the throat. I hate to break a promise to her, but know I won't wear it. I figure I can give it to snappy-dressing Frank to accessorize with. I can't imagine what the X-ray technician will think as my luggage sets off the metal detectors.

"Rock stars have to carry a lot of baggage—I hope that suitcases are the only kind of 'baggage' you'll ever have in your life," Mama says, proud of her analogy.

I grab two Double Stuf Oreos and sit at the kitchen table as Mama rolls the last suitcase into the dining room.

"Can I help?" I ask, as I unscrew the chocolate cookie sandwich and scrape the thick, sweet white icing off with my front teeth.

"That's okay, honey. Just about got it whipped," Mama replies with a sing-song sigh of relief. She lays her hands on my shoulders and kneads my aching muscles. "I love you, bub. I'm so glad that your dad gets to go with you to Sweden. You know I wish I could be there, too, but I'm sure you and your father are going to have the time of your lives.

"I know you feel as though Dad doesn't care about your music, but he's excited—Dad just wants the best for you…truth be told, he's really nervous for you, "she explains.

"I know, Mama. I just can't help feeling that he's really disappointed with me for missing the football game. We've been working toward that game for all these years. I know it's Dad's dream," I voice quietly.

"Sweetie, we just want you to follow your dreams. Your dreams are our dreams. We're with you one hundred percent, whether you're a football player, a musician, a mechanic—whatever. Dad and I are so proud of the young man you've become and all that you're going to do. We love you so much," Mama assures as she wipes back a curl that had fallen in front of my tired eyes. "Now, go get ready for bed. We've gotta get you and Daddy to the airport by six thirty a.m.—I know, not rocker-friendly hours. I already bought the Red Bull," she chimes, slightly pleased with herself for her contribution of remembering every last detail of the packing process.

I stand up and bear-hug Mama. I lift her off her feet. She screams for me to put her down. As I do, she spins me around like a drill sergeant.

"All right, down the hall you go. G'night, babe. I'll see you bright and early."

"You mean dark and early. Thanks for packing for us Mama...love you," I say tenderly.

"You're welcome, son. Love you, too," she smiles. Teardrops well up and pool above Mama's bottom lashes. She blinks and her tears make tiny falling rivers that wet her flushed cheeks. I don't think they're sad tears, though. More like "my baby's growing up" tears. I sure love my Mama.

I'm exhausted, but have so much on my mind, including worrying if I'll be able to sleep. The trip is going to be so thrilling, but nerve-racking at the same time. I can feel the tension of knowing that I'm going to be a world away, almost literally, from my comfort zone. My life feels like a thousand-piece jigsaw puzzle that's been dumped out on the floor.

I'm starting with the middle pieces, the ones where all the color and shape just blends together. Most kids my age are still working on the borders—the straight edges—the easy part.

As confused as I am, I'm more suited to the challenge of starting in the center. I never wade into the frigid water at Baron Fork Creek in the springtime. I just bail right in. And I'm usually the first one of my buddies to take a dare, so I guess I'm pretty suited for this life. I'm ready to jump off the bluff, feet first, into the icy current without hesitation. I'm excited to start the puzzle from the inside out. It's not always easy, but it's more satisfying when the picture is complete.

As I enter my room for the evening, I rub my tired eyes and look around. It can clearly be seen that my domain is a house divided. One side of my room is dedicated to the Coweta Tigers. On the shelves and walls are orange and black pennants dotted with tiger paws, gold plaques, trophies, and certificates from my athletic achievements over the years.

The other side of my room is plastered with posters of rock legends. Led Zeppelin, Pink Floyd, Pantera and, of course, Metallica, are a few of the bands displayed. I also have magazine cutouts of some of my favorite new bands: Needtobreathe, The Foo Fighters, and The Zac Brown Band, to name a few. They're each a source of inspiration to me. They all influence my musical style and writing.

My custom San Dimas guitar and my Boulder

Creek acoustic hang securely on my bedroom wall. Betty is in the steadfast grip of a special hanger that looks like a giant silver hand jutting out of the wall from a square wooden block.

I pull my Gibson gal down and strum her silver strings. The liquid metal sound fills my ears and puts me solely in the moment at hand. I begin to play the Coweta Tigers fight song. I've never played our school song on a guitar before. It sounds so puny compared to the Tiger marching band's spirit-rousting version.

My fingers settle still on the strings. My thoughts drift to Sophie. I'm going miss her next week. As I return my Gibson to its hanger, my BlackBerry alerts me to a text message. I can't believe it—it's from Sophie!

Hey, Forrest! I just wanna wish ya luck in Sweden at your KISS show. Still can't believe your gonna get to open for them. my dads freakin out! :) I know youll be amazing!! call me when ya get back—maybe we can hang out...OK? <3

A feeling of warmth spreads through my chest. Sophie has signed off with a heart next to her name. I text her back, hesitating as I type so that I can search for the perfect words.

thank u soooo much, Sophie...thanx for bein there for me...Im glad weve gotten to know each other better the past few weeks...see ya when I get back. Id love to hang! I'll call ya for sure! :) Forrest

I push the send button on my phone and watch the tiny envelope icon rotate and disappear on my cell screen. I know in my heart that Sophie and I have both made it official—we're falling for each other.

I dread my next text. It's to Heather. She's not been around much, which leads me to suspect that that she's hooking up with someone else. She won't break up with me, though, because of all the media attention me and my band are getting. I know she's using me. Right now, being with me gives her popularity points at school. I'm definitely going to end it with her as soon as I get back from Sweden. I begin to type:

hey, Heather! just wanted to say gdnight. see ya when I get bk from Sweden. Hope ya have a good week. Forrest

It takes several minutes, and the return text from Heather reads, **Oh, hey! have a good time Forrest...YOU ROCK! :)**

"You rock?" I whisper to myself—how cliché—how Heather.

I set my trusty Superman alarm clock for the unholy, donut-making hour of 5:30 a.m. and nestle into my cozy, soft blankets. Mama washed my sheets today. They smell fresh, like Aunt Carmen's meadow in the springtime. My fuzzy fleece blanket crackles and sparks tiny purple static electricity lights as I pull the warm cover up over my cold ears. I'm so grateful for the things my mom and dad do for me. My eyelids become heavy. My soul feels content. I whisper a prayer for a safe trip, for my dad to have a good time, and for my teammates to have a great game.

I slide my iPod off my night stand and put my ear buds in. Ray Charles' lonely crooning lulls me to sleep. Tonight I dream of being on stage with KISS. We're playing the blues—the stage is explosive, with Gene Simmons breathing orange, bellowing, volumes of fire. Randy and Heather are in the background having a pie-eating contest at the Coweta Fall Festival. My dream is completely random, and totally awesome.

CHAPTER EIGHTEEN

I'm always on time—on time to school, on time to football, on time to band practice, gigs, etc. I'm always on time to the airport as well. This isn't the case for Jake, Randy and Cody. My bandmates, God love 'em, are chronic late arrivers, and this morning is no exception. Of course, they all overslept.

I look up to see them making their way to the baggage check line. They resemble long-haired, brain-seeking zombies. Their pale faces are expressionless as they slowly shuffle their feet toward the airline attendant.

"Dude, one of these days you guys are gonna miss the boat," I state in frustration. "Late, late, late! Duuudes, you guys are ALWAYS LATE!"

"Hey, man, it's all good. We got an extra hour of sleep," Jake boasts.

"I wonder if we'll ever have to take a boat." Cody ponders.

Randy opens his mouth wide, expelling an exaggerated a.m. yawn. "Yeah dude, don't be such a time warden, Forrest." He pops the tab on his Diet Mountain Dew. It spews everywhere—I shake my head.

After a vice grip hug and kiss, and then another hug, and another kiss, my dad and I say our goodbyes to Mama and Megan. Megan informs me that I have to know she loves me a lot because she got up at 5:30 in the morning to see me off. I banter back that the only reason she got up early was so she could go to Sticky Buns Donut Shop on the way home—and then I call her a fatty.

"Bring me back somethin' good!" she accepts my good natured insult with a grin.

"And take lots and lots of pictures!" Mama adds. Her fingers are laced nervously together.

As Dad and I step across the security check line, Mama raises her hand. She makes Aunt Carmen's "rock" sign. She's saying I love you in sign language. I sign "I love you" back. We turn and wave three more times before disappearing through the gate to board the plane.

My chest tightens. I feel like I'm boarding a NASA shuttle for the moon. It'll be a ten hour flight. Dad and I thought we were going to get to sit by each other, but he's seated four rows up with the MTV film crew that's accompanying us. Unfortunately, I'm stuck sitting next to a man named

Buddy, who is a very large and obnoxious man. Buddy snorts as he laughs at all of his not-so-funny jokes, and smells like stale Cheez-Its.

Luckily, seated on the other side of me is a very pretty young woman. She's dressed comfy for the flight in black yoga pants, a pink t-shirt and grey ballet flats. Her name is Gretchen and she tells me that she's returning home to Sweden after visiting some of her family in the U.S. I find her charming and very interesting, easy to make small talk with.

Gretchen has actually heard of Cellar Door Is Gone in Sweden and knows our song, "Rocket." She's thrilled to hear the story behind my band, and even has a cousin who's actually going to the KISS concert in Stockholm.

It truly is a small world after all, I think.

During the tedious flight, Buddy keeps butting in on our conversation. He brags about being a "fine wine connoisseur," but drinks beer most of the flight. Buddy thinks it is priceless comedy when he asks the flight attendant for a Hiney. "That's short for Heineken," he hee-haws. "Get it?" The stewardess rolls her cart and her eyes as she continues forward.

I have to let Buddy squeeze by me every thirty minutes or so for a bathroom break, which becomes ever so annoying. Cody looks up from his Sky Mall catalogue as the brash comedian lumbers down the aisle for his fourth potty break. Buddy's crack is half exposed, thanks to his oversized, stretchy elastic-waist pants.

"Looks more like he's a connoisseur of sweat

pants," Cody comments casually, before going back to making out his airline catalogue Christmas list.

The sarcastic comment isn't lost on Gretchen and me and we giggle groggily. We're all very relieved when Buddy finally passes out, five hours into the flight—that is until he starts snoring.

I put my headphones on to block out the nasal-knocking sound of Buddy sawing logs. The song, "Slow Ride," by Fog Hat, is cued up. I shift in my seat. My rear end is numb. I cover my upper body with the minute blue square of sterile cloth that is the airline blanket. I'm on a "slow ride" to Sweden.

After two long naps, three meals, eight water bottles, two cranberry juices, and three in-flight movies, the plane touches down with a landing fit for balancing eggs. I bid my new international friend, Gretchen, goodbye, and autograph a cocktail napkin per her request.

Buddy even wishes me luck. He says he'll Google me, and snorts one last belly laugh, accidentally shooting a salted peanut out of his mouth. I'm so glad the flight is over. We're finally at our international destination.

Sweden is beautiful, bright and green. As we leave our hotel room later that day to go sightseeing, the lights, TV, and everything else that you would turn off before you leave your room shuts down automatically when the door locks behind us. Dad and I are impressed by their innovative energy conservation ideas. I can already sense the trip has been good for Dad, who's never been more than one state away from Oklahoma. He's all smiles. He looks several years younger as we talk about all that is interesting in this city. A city that's a world away from our country community.

We explore the town of Stockholm, which is filled with quaint shops and interesting, old architecture. There are also a lot of beautiful fair-haired girls in the city. Several of them remind me of Sophie. I suspect that she must have Swedish relatives in her family tree somewhere.

I also spot a girl who reminds me of Heather. She's a spoiled American tourist who's clearly agitated by the communication barrier as she tries to order lunch—a very pretty girl with a very ugly attitude.

Jake, Randy, Cody, and I decide it's time to try the local cuisine. We have absolutely no idea what we're ordering off the menu. When our meals arrive, we still don't have a clue what we're about to eat. Dad's the lucky one—he scores chicken. I'm not so fortunate—I get pork. Not pork chops, or pork ribs. It's a gelatinous blob of pork knuckle that doesn't stop jiggling for at least five seconds after the waitress sets it on the table in front of me.

The other boys get pickled herring, covered in a white sauce, and a slab of raw, pink salmon on the side. We feel like we're on *Fear Factor* as we dare each other to take bites of the mystery meals.

Our attitude is that if life hands you lemons, you make lemonade. Then you go to the Swedish McDonalds and eat real food!

My bandmates and I step into the best joke ever as we step off the trolley. Randy points out a street sign that reads, "Ut Fart." Apparently, "Fart" translates to "speed" in English! The signs are at each entrance and exit of the parking garages. We have a field day with this. We snap pictures of all of us pointing and laughing. Cody has the best pose. He backs up to the sign and puts his finger to his lips like, "oopsie."

Mama sent her arsenal of cameras and camcorders with Dad and made him take a sacred oath to capture as much of the trip as he could.

Dad and I find the perfect souvenir shop, and buy Mama and Megan each a small, ceramic, red-suited gnome. The chubby, snow-bearded, elf-like statues are everywhere. Our two little quaint elves will soon have a new home in a flower garden in Cow-Town Oklahoma.

After an exhausting day of sightseeing, we settle back into our hotel rooms. I'm Jonesin' for my BlackBerry, but since cell phones would cost an arm and a leg to use from Sweden, I set up my laptop and webcam so we can talk to Mama and Megan courtesy of the hotel's Wi-Fi. It's so comforting to see their faces as they sit around our big oak kitchen table back home. Our dog, Stella, even licks the camera.

After saying goodnight to Mama and Megan, I go to Sophie's Facebook page and ask her to get on her webcam so we can chat. Sophie and I stay on our computers for over three hours, talking. Dad unknowingly walks by the webcam sporting his new gnome-printed boxer shorts. Sophie and I laugh until we cry.

It's so ironic that it took my leaving the country for Sophie and me to learn so much about each other. The internet is a wonderful thing.

Dad says it's time for bed, and starts giving me the old, "When I was young" speech. He explains that he and Mama managed to meet, date and even get married, all without the benefit of cell phones or computers. "Mama even lived way out in the boondocks—twenty miles out on bad dirt road." He declares with a sense of pride that he snagged her like a prize coon.

Dad can't help but laugh when I ask him if he had to track her. "Look for broken twigs and Appaloosa hoof prints, did ya?" I tease.

"No sir. I had a land line and an old Ford pickup truck—worked just fine!" Dad says. I still can't imagine functioning socially on a day-to-day basis without the benefit of texting or Facebook—never ever!

I beg Dad for another twenty minutes, and me and Sophie's marathon conversation continues. We find out we have a lot in common—from music, to family life, to religious beliefs. Sophie isn't into the party scene either. She's not a goody-two-shoes; she's just a good girl, and I'm so glad we've gotten to know each other better.

My Mac laptop is the bomb. It brought Sophie up close and personal to me from thousands of miles away. I can't wait to get back to Coweta, Oklahoma to give her a non-virtual hug!

CHAPTER NINETEEN

The big day is finally here. My band and I will be sharing the stage tonight with the one and only rock legends, KISS. I think our dads and Jake's Uncle Walt are almost as nervous as the boys and I are as we make our way to the Olympic Stadium in Stockholm.

This is the venue that housed the 1912 Olympic Games and now, my band, Cellar Door Is Gone, is going to open for KISS in this historic structure. We're in awe. I'm overcome by a sudden, heavy feeling in my stomach that quickly turns into burning nausea. I have an immediate desire to chug Pepto-Bismol. All the excitement and apprehension are actually good feelings, though. I know that I'm about to do something bigger than I've ever done in my life, and so does my gut. Reality has hit home big time.

The boys and I make our way to our modest dressing room once the doors of the stadium are opened. Rabid Swedish rock fans swarm in, and race for the prime real estate at the front of the gigantic stage. Once again we have to pinch ourselves to make sure we're not dreaming. This time, I pinch Jake!

The show promoter greets us with a shocked expression as we enter the "once again not green" green room.

"Are you guys the band from the States?" he asks, with hesitation. His coarse, bushy grey eyebrows, that look like they have a life of their own, raise with a skeptical arch.

I step up as the band's spokesman, answering quickly and confidently.

"Yep—I mean—umm, yes sir we are."

"You have *got* to be kidding me. How old are you boys?" the promoter asks with proper and pronounced accent. Aggravation is sketched all over his face.

"I'm sixteen, and the rest of the boys are fifteen," I say, throwing my head back toward my bandmates, who stand motionless.

"I do not know *what* the booking agent was thinking! We are going to have over thirty-thousand fans ready for a rock show. Can you boys handle that?" The promoter inquires.

"Oh...definitely. We promise we won't let you down," I return. I stand with my shoulders and back straight, thinking that if I could add another inch to my height, it would add more credibility to our band.

"Okay, boys. You will be meeting KISS in thirty minutes. You had better get a move on. I will have my assistant come get you for the meeting in the press room, okay?" The promoter informs us slowly and clearly as if we're second graders.

"Remember, over thirty thousand fans, so be in top form," he instructs staunchly.

"We'll be just fine," I assure him. Then I turn to my bandmates and echo, "just fine!" I speak with conviction, but inside, my stomach is doing back flips. I'm now officially a nervous wreck.

It's finally time for our meeting with KISS—the most surreal moment of my life. Two days ago I was in Cow-Town, Oklahoma, population seven thousand. I was playing football and practicing with my band in a barn. Now I'm getting ready to meet one of the biggest acts in rock history. I'm minutes away from meeting the legendary Gene Simmons. I'm suddenly pale with apprehension about being face-to-face with the literally white-faced KISS!

Two muscle bound security guards escort us to KISS's well-watched and very private dressing room. I realize that I've been holding my breath for at least a minute. I exhale and inhale deeply to calm myself, and they enter. The boys and I shake their hands with respect, as camera flashes pop. I step alongside Gene Simmons. My dad thankfully keeps his cool long enough to get a quick pic of me and my band with the super cool legends of rock.

KISS is truly larger than life. The killer platform boots they wear on stage have them towering at least twelve inches over us. My heart is pumping double-time as I let Gene Simmons know what an unbelievable honor it will be to be standing on the same stage as them. Our dads stand frozen in ecstatic shock. They have dumb-founded smiles plastered across their faces. The boys and I stand with the familiar rock grimaces on our faces as we pose with KISS in all their painted glory.

After the photo, Tommy Thayer shakes my hand again and gives me an ultra-cool wink, and Paul Stanley actually gives me one of his signed picks to add to my collection. I'm almost speechless, but manage to choke out a goofy laugh and a, "Thank you sooo much—you guys are freaking amazing!"

KISS is very gracious, but also very much in demand. The superstar group is quickly whisked out of the white green room to go back to the mystical place that only KISS goes.

"DUDE…WE JUST MET KISS!!!" the boys and I yell as we jump up and down in place with our arms around each other like giddy grade school girls. It's unbelievable—the coolest experience of my life!

After the meet-and-greet, the leery promoter, and his bushy eyebrows, leads us to the back of the stage, giving us time to finish setting up our gear. I'm still in a star-struck haze as I hop up on a riser to get my set list. I'm not paying attention to my step. The next thing I know, I lose my footing and find myself falling through the thick, black velvet curtain that keeps us hidden from the audience. I'm now smack dab in the middle of the sprawling stage. I'm mortified and frozen solid.

The scene from *The Wizard of Oz* where Toto pulls back the long, veiled curtain, revealing the Great and Mighty Oz, pops into my head. Dude...I'm definitely not in Kansas—or Oklahoma, for that matter—anymore!

My feet are cemented to the floor as I gawk at the thousands of fans in the arena. In the midst of feeling like a fool, and wondering what my escape plan is going be, I hear one lone voice with a foreign accent yell, "Hey, it is Forrrrest!"

I instinctively wave as I scramble to get back behind the amps. I frantically muddle through the curtain fabric, eventually finding the escape hatch. As I jump up, the crowd goes nuts. I can't believe my ears. They're actually cheering!

"Are you okay?" Dad yells over the crowd noise. He grabs my arm and helps me back behind the stage.

"I almost peed my pants!" I wail, my voice shaking.

"You're gonna be just fine. Sounds like they already know who you are!" Dad says, chuckling. His expression turns serious and honest. "Son, I'm so proud of you. This is far more exciting than any football game I've ever been to." He continues, in a tone that's meant to keep me calm, "Forrest, you boys are gonna knock 'em dead. Deep breaths, son!" My father's warm smile and confident words give me much needed comfort. I suddenly feel confident and the feeling that I swallowed a brick begins to dissolve away.

Dad clasps my shaking hands in his large, steady ones, closes his eyes and says a prayer for a great show. For the first time, I notice large calluses on my dad's hands from years of handling boxes for UPS and working at my grandpa's farm. His calluses are just like the ones on Coach Bryan's hands. I respect my dad more than I can say. "Do good!" he says. Dad gives me one last embrace and then walks me toward the stage ramp.

I can feel my heartbeat begin to readjust to a normal rhythm. I'm thankful for my strong father and his faith in me. I repeat my favorite Bible verse in my head: *"I can do all things through Christ who strengthens me." I can do this.*

I grab my trusty Gibson Girl Betty—I'm now ready to step, not fall, back onto the stage.

CHAPTER TWENTY

There's no turning back. We're about to seal our fate. Either we'll rock hard or fall hard like a rock. The boys and I man our respective rock stations that are marked by silver duct tape "X"s. My legs feel heavy. My hands are weak. I take one last swig from my water bottle and toss it to Dad. My mouth immediately becomes sandpaper dry again. *Deep breaths*, I repeat silently to myself.

I make my way to the isolated microphone stand at the front of the stage. I feel dizzy. The crowd of over thirty-five thousand enthusiastic Swedes begins to roar. MTV cameras circle around my head, cords snake at my feet. I hear buzzing, whistling, clapping. It's all a blur.

I scream, "*Hur mar du Stockholm*?" the Swedish phrase for, "How are you, Stockholm?" into the mic and raise both fists in the air to show I'm totally fired up and ready to rock.

The roar is deafening. It literally makes my chest rumble. The old adrenaline kicks in, and the blood in my veins pumps like premium gasoline. I stand for what seems like an eternity, waiting for Cody to click his drumsticks and cue up our first song. All I hear is the noise of the crowd and the thud of my heartbeat in my brain. I turn to face Cody. He's frozen behind his drum kit like a deer in headlights.

"Let's *rock* this mother, Cody!" I scream over my shoulder. To my great relief, he snaps out of his paralyzed trance. Cody cracks his wooden sticks together and crashes the cymbals.

"Are you REEAAAADY TO ROOOCK?" I wail into the microphone.

It's all history from there. My blood pressure regulates, I find my groove. The music flows out of me with ease and liquidity. My vocals are heavy and on key. I feel my fingers tread fast and sure on the strings of my guitar. It's like an out-of-body experience for me as I draw energy from the massive, partying crowd. We're all in this together. I can feel the recycling of excitement between the audience and my band. The Swedish fans adore us.

The last song of our set is a cover of Pink Floyd's, "Brick in the Wall." At least twenty thousand Swedes chant with me, singing along with their hands in the air. I'm commanding a rock-n-roll army—me, a sixteen-year-old kid who, this time last week, had to fight for a chance to get a word in edgewise at my school cafeteria lunch table. In stark contrast to the crazy chaos of the thundering music, a multi-colored hot air balloon drifts lazily over the stage. Surprisingly, as cool as a cucumber, I lift my finger to the clouds.

"Say hello to the people in the *sky*!" I converse with the crowd as they roar even louder. I feel so right at home, here in my thirty minutes of rock-n-roll heaven.

Our last song winds down like the final lap of a NASCAR race in North Carolina. All that's missing is the smell of burned rubber. I bolt straight up, jetting several feet off the ground. I float with my guitar. The neck slices through the electrified air as I land. I jump two more times as Cody gives the final blow on his drum kit. Randy and Jake squeal out their last note for continuous reverb. My boots land back on stage in perfect, synchronized time to the last metal-tinged crash of Cody's Gretch cymbals. We've officially courted the crowd.

And next I utter my final words of the set before the boys and I wander, sweaty and spent, off the stage: "UP NEXT...KISS!!!!!!!" I can now die a happy boy.

There's no doubt in my mind as I hear the crowd chant, "Cellar Door's Gone—Cellar Door's Gone," this is what I'm destined to do for the rest of my life. The victorious feeling pulsing through my body can't be bottled. You can't smell it. You can't taste it. A million dollars can't buy it. But it's real. It's palpable. And at this moment, it's all mine.

The boys and I collapse into our families' arms. Frank is in full meltdown mode. I'm afraid for a moment that we might have to call a paramedic for him as he clutches the brass buttons on his fancy black coat.

"That was THEEEE STUFF, boys!" Frank huffs, out of breath from excitement. "Now let's get you lads to the merch tent."

As I jog with my dad past the chain link fence that separates us from the crowd, a pack of young girls gathers, screaming my name. They tug at my shirt and grab at my hair.

A long line of newly-made fans snakes around until it reaches our merch tent. Beautiful Swedish girls blush as they ask for our autographs in their best English.

In the middle of the confusion, Dad looks at me in disbelief. He cups his hands over his mouth, forming a makeshift megaphone. "Hey, bud...if you need a backup singer, I'm available," he jokes, his eyes twinkling.

"Easy there, Mick Jagger," I tease. Dad smiles and gives me a Vulcan grip on the neck.

The show promoter comes over to shake our hands. He's blown away by our performance. I can tell he's been nipping at the vodka bottle in the green room, as his words are slurred. The tipsy promo man tells us that he would be honored to work with us again anytime.

He grabs my hand and asks his final question. "Are you boys really from *Cowtown*, Oklahoma?

That is *priceless*! I love it!" The promoter howls. He continues to belly laugh as he teeters back and forth, ultimately disappearing into the thick, bustling crowd.

Dad approaches the table as I sign my last poster. He picks up a black Cellar Door Is Gone t-shirt from the disheveled pile and holds it up to his chest.

"Looks like you have my size after all," he says, as he pulls the hip tee printed with my band's logo over his orange polo shirt.

"Dad...I couldn't have done any of this without you. I'm so glad you came with me."

I hug my dad so tightly that I think I might pull him right through me. His return embrace is just as strong.

"I wouldn't have missed it for the world, son," Dad replies sincerely, "not for the world."

Knowing that my dad supports my dream lifts a worrisome weight from my shoulders. His words of acceptance mean everything to me. The wedge between us has been chiseled away.

All four of us boys compress ourselves into the van for our return trip to the hotel. We still feel steamy from our rock-n-roll workout. Randy pipes up, and to no one's surprise, he asks if we can go back to McDonalds for cheeseburgers and fries.

Cody's monotone voice drifts from the back seat of the stuffy van, as dry as a bone. He jokes that Swedish food is like Chinese food.

"Dang pickled herring...eat it, and you're hungry again in an hour!"

CHAPTER TWENTY ONE

Our appearance in Sweden is deemed a huge success. Sweden loves Cellar Door Is Gone, and Cellar Door Is Gone loves Sweden. It has been a once in a lifetime experience for us all. Now, it's time to board the jet for the slow ride back to Cow-Town.

Dad and I are both exhausted and exhilarated. Our grueling flight will be touching down in Tulsa just an hour or so before my team's State Championship game. I'm drained and cranky. The thought of not playing in the game suddenly begins to eat at me. Pangs of regret start to needle me.

Mama is waiting for Dad and me as we make our way through the terminal. She is decked out in her Coweta Tigers orange and black, and of course, her Cellar Door Is Gone ball cap. Tears stream out of Mama's big brown eyes as she grabs us up in a tight welcome home embrace. From the strength of her grip, I can easily tell how glad she is to have us home.

"We missed you guys so much!" Mama gushes. Her tears melt into a huge grin when she sees that Dad is actually wearing a Cellar Door Is Gone t-shirt. Mama squeezes Dad's hand and hugs him close in affectionate approval.

Jake, Randy, Cody and I all share a Cellar Door Is Gone group hug and round of nuks. They even say they're going to the game. We all can't wait to share the details of our trip with our friends at school. But I doubt I'll see them there. Like Randy says—they're rockers not jocks.

My emotions are bottoming out from lack of sleep. "This sucks." I mumble. I realize immediately that it was the wrong thing to say, as Mama snaps her head around.

"Excuse me?" Mama says in a questioning tone as she takes two casual steps back to stand by my side so that all of her words will land directly into my ear.

"I'm sorry, but it's just not fair that I have to miss playing in the game." I try to defend.

By the look on Mama's face I know it's not sympathy that I'm about to receive. I'm about to get reprimanded big time.

Mama stares straight ahead and begins to speak as though she's discussing the airport décor. "Young man…where have you been this week?" she asks.

"Sweden." I respond in a "no duh" kind of way.

"And just what did you do there?" she continues with great annunciation.

"Played a show." My answer is not the detailed response that Mama was shooting for.

"And who did you play a show with?" Mama asks through her teeth.

"KISS," I concede.

"Hmmm..." Mama says. "Well...that happens every day, huh?"

I begin to feel pretty ashamed of myself. "No ma'am, it doesn't," I mumble.

"Forrest, we are going to the game as a family, and you are going to be there for your team—okay?" Mama asks.

"Got it!" I return boldly. My words have dual purpose, as I grab the handle of my guitar case just before it gets sucked back into the black hole of the luggage carousel. Betty is safely back in my possession. I feel whole again.

"Good." Mama finalizes the discussion.

"Hey, Mama, check this out." I unfasten the laminated KISS, all-access backstage pass that hangs from my wallet chain.

"Pretty dang cool." Mama smiles as I hand it to her.

"Dad has one, too," I continue.

"Yep, I was a V.I.P." Dad smiles.

"You guys better have taken hundreds of pictures," Mama lectures, pointing her finger at Dad. "Now let's get a move on, boys. The game's already started," Mama declares. "Everyone in town is dying to hear about your KISS show. You know Forrest, you and the boys are hometown heroes."

I grab our last piece of luggage from the baggage carousel and forge on like a soldier. I'm ready to go root my team on.

As I enter the buzzing stadium, I'm swamped with townsfolk shaking my hand and patting me on the back. If I'm asked how the trip was once, I'm asked fifty times. I can only repeat in simple words that it was the coolest experience of my entire life.

The continuous showering of heartfelt good wishes is wonderful, but I still feel a bit of jealousy that I'm not out on the field. I quickly shake it out of my head, though. I've just lived the dream of a lifetime. I need to cheer my brothers out on the field to victory.

I grab a large Coke at the concession booth, that I get for free from the booster club moms, and make my way through the crowd into the noisy stands. It's the third quarter of the game and the score is tied: twenty-seven to twenty-seven. I suddenly realize that I've never been to a school function in my "rock-n-roll uniform." I feel out of place in my skin-tight, jet black jeans, silver stud belt, wrist bands, and weathered, black leather jacket as I begin doing the old "excuse me...pardon me...excuse me," throughout my assent up the overcrowded metal bleachers.

I gingerly make my way past Mr. Franklin, an

elder from my church. The frail gentleman stands up to let me pass. He adjusts his orange Coweta Tigers ball cap and gives me a slight sideways glance. For a moment I think that he might be judging me because of the bold look I'm sporting among the sea of conservative school spirit attire. I stand out like a sore thumb—a sore thumb in a black leather glove.

To my surprise, he has just the opposite reaction. "Come on by here, Rock Star!" Mr. Franklin states boldly, as he pats me on the shoulder. "How was the trip, young man?" he questions, extending his boney, feeble right hand.

"Unbelievable—it was just amazing!" I return, nodding in respect.

"Oh, that's just wonderful! Ruth and I are so proud of you boys. You've been blessed with a lot of talent...and opening for KISS...well that's just the bees' knees! We're all alookin' forward to ya playing at the church again real soon. We sure miss ya on the football field tonight, but the team's doin' a fine job, just fine. Well, I'll let ya get to your seat. Take care, son."

I'm so grateful for his kind words. The generation gap is closed a bit tighter tonight, thanks to KISS and the Coweta Tigers.

Megan jumps up and down and waves wildly to me in the jam-packed bleachers. "Heeey, bub!" Megan yells over the cheers of the football fanatics. She gives me a big sisterly hug before I take a seat in the ice cold bleachers. I pull my fitted jacket collar closer around my neck to block the biting wind. I'm grateful for the orange and black plaid afghan that Megan has laid down. I take a seat next to her on it.

"Oooh, look at you in your leather! You look soooo hot, bub!" Megan beams, half teasing. "So how was it?" she asks, shaking my arm.

"Oh, man, Megan. Words can't even describe how amazing it was. Meeting KISS was freaking incredible, and Sweden was soooo beautiful. Me and Dad wish you and Mom could've been there, but we took tons of pictures." I wrinkle my nose. "The only thing I would've changed was the food. I'm totally ready for some good old Split Rail BBQ and Taco Bell for sure!"

I settle in the stands with my family and join the spirited home crowd in cheering on the Tigers. Kyle is having the game of his career, but D.J. is a little off. I could swear that he's giving me dirty looks from the sidelines. Maybe it's just my imagination, but I think I am receiving way too much attention for his liking as usual.

"Foooorest…hey, Forrest!" Heather's shrill voice drifts up sharply from the field. She's spotted me. Heather blows me a kiss and waves to me like a beauty queen in a parade.

I have a flashback of our elementary school talent show when Heather's talent was demonstrating a "pageant wave." Ironically, her cheerleading skirt is almost as short as the little, sparkling pageant dress that she wore in second grade.

"Well, well, well," Megan chimes slyly. Miss Heather doesn't think you'll find out what she's been up to while you were gone," she continues as she shakes her head.

"Oh...hit me," I'm sure I know what she's been up to, but I'm anxious to hear the cold hard facts first hand from my sis.

"Heather and D.J. spent the week party-hoppin' together. Let's just say I saw them getting very cozy at the Quick Trip the other night. She should really put the top up on her convertible when she's playing 'kissy-face.' Not too discreeeet!" my sister sings out.

"Dude, Megan. You just made my night." I high five my sis. Relief runs through me. Now I can finally get *rid* of Heather once and for all without feeling guilty.

Not wanting to waste any more time on relationship drama, I turn my focus to the Tiger marching band and spot Sophie right away. I stand and wave my arms in all directions, trying to get her attention. Sophie sees me. She waves back. Her broadening smile illuminates the band bleachers. I survey the height of the fence and decide I'm going to hop over it as soon as the game is over—I'm going to make a path straight for Sophie.

I turn my concentration back to the very close game; I yell until my veins pop in my temples as the opposing team runs the ball down to our ten yard line. The score is still tied, twenty-seven to twenty-seven. I begin to bite the jagged cuticles on my nails.

"COME ON TIGERS! HOLD EM'!" I wail. I stand up and stomp my feet on the clanging metal bleachers. I feel completely helpless. Trying to encourage my teammates from the stands is frustrating. I'd give anything to be on the field blocking.

Relief comes over me as the Tigers' defense makes a crucial tackle on the fourth down, stopping our rival's forward progress. The football is set sailing with a thud as it's punted. Now it's up to the Tigers to get the ball over the goal line. The time clock is ticking relentlessly, with only two minutes left to go in the game. My stomach is in knots.

On the field, my team huddles for their final time-out. I know D.J.'s best decision is a pass to the end zone to Kyle. The other team's defensive coverage of the receivers had gotten weak due to an injury during the last play. D.J. appears to be distracted by Heather and the smiles and waves she's directing toward me in the stands. I can see that he's fuming. He's certainly not giving the game the attention it needs, especially on the critical last downs at hand.

I can see the formation D.J. has called. It looks like he's going try to go for a quarterback keeper. I know D.J. well enough to sense he wants full credit for scoring the winning touchdown. It's clear, even from here in the stands, that there's now an "I" in team, as far as D.J. is concerned.

CHAPTER TWENTY TWO

Two quick plays later, the Tigers aren't gaining much ground. D.J. still refuses to throw the ball to Kyle, even though he's been wide open near the goal line. I have a sneaking suspicion he won't let Kyle have the ball because Kyle's my best friend. I'm sure D.J. is still holding a grudge because of Kyle's cut down after Box tackled me. Instead of an athletic leader, D.J. has become a manipulative dictator.

D.J. reluctantly hands the ball off to his running back, but the defensive line is too beefy. The play is squelched after only a gain of a yard. The Tigers now have the ball on the fifteen-yard line. Dad and I scream until we're blue in the face for D.J. to pass Kyle the ball. I can see Kyle screaming at D.J., too.

The Tigers huddle for their last time-out. D.J. opens his mouth and rebels, the steam from the cold night air puffing out of his mouth. He looks like a mad, fire-breathing dragon. Even D.J.'s dull-witted friend Box shakes his head in agreement with Kyle. I can hear the burly center snorting at him to pass Kyle the ball. It doesn't matter what the team or coaches want at this point—D.J.'s mind is made up.

"Sixteen on two...sixteen on two!" D.J. commands. He ignores the coach's orders as the team reluctantly breaks from the huddle before a delay of game penalty is called. It's too late for anyone to dispute the call as D.J. belts out, "Sixteen...sixteen...hut, hut!!"

Helmets crack as the spent linemen begin to block for D.J., who selfishly holds onto the ball. He finds a small rabbit hole and breaks from the crumbling line of scrimmage. He sprints, dodging the first defender, but a solid-as-a-rock linebacker on the opposing team nearly picks D.J. up and throws him down. The violent crack is audible into the top seats of the stands. The football sails out of D.J.'s hands before he hits the frigid, hard, unforgiving turf.

We all hold our breath collectively as the pigskin pops out of D.J.'s flailing arms. The entire home bleachers have all but chalked the game up as a loss. The most important game of the past eight years comes to a bitter close. We all gasp and begin to exhale in unison in gut wrenching disappointment.

The rickety scoreboard clock ticks off the last three seconds of the game without mercy. There's no way to stop it. Three…two…one…and, lo and behold, out of the crowd of grass-stained jerseys, Kyle leaps into the air and secures the barreling football. He lands with both feet churning like the Road Runner and turns for the goal line, four treacherous yards away.

The opposing team grabs in vain at his un-tucked shirt-tail, but Kyle is able to shuck off two defenders as he closes in on the two-yard line.

I'm on my feet, going crazy. I'm so pumped that I feel dizzy. "GO KYLE! GET IN THERE!" I scream, trying to will my buddy across the goal line.

Kyle shakes off the last defensive player and, as the horn buzzes signifying the end of the game, he leaps into the end zone, hits the ground, and rolls twice.

Kyle stands slowly and deliberately. He displays, for all to see, the football still secure in his gloved hands. My best friend has just scored the winning touchdown for the Tigers. My team has just won the coveted State Championship title!

The Tiger fans go ballistic. I see purple dots and get a full-on head rush from screaming so loud. Megan's popcorn flies in every direction as she jumps up and down. Mom and Dad's stadium seats fall backwards. Cowbells clank. The home side bleachers turn into celebration central. What a barn burner. The Tiger players and coaches are ecstatic.

Everyone is elated—everyone, that is, except

for D.J. He looks completely dejected. Instead of celebrating with his team, D.J. takes off his black scuffed helmet and walks around in a daze, like it's the end of the world and he is the sole survivor. He appears to be all alone in a crowd of hundreds. His teammates are less than happy with him. Even his partner in crime, Sam the Box, gives D.J. the cold shoulder pad.

They all know good and well that D.J.'s petty jealousy and big ego had almost cost them the most important game of the year—the most important game of their lifetime.

Kyle, on the other hand, is the man of the hour. He looks like a steel orb in a pinball machine as he bounces randomly above the shoulders of his fellow football players. On the ground, he's mauled with bear hugs and helmet slaps. My gridiron buddies and I are on top of the world!

I scan the field, desperately looking for Sophie. The marching band is in the middle of the school fight song, and I can see her laughing from fifty yards away.

I can barely wait to hug Sophie, but there's one thing I have to take care of first. Turning to Mama, who's still in full celebration mode, I ask for the KISS backstage pass that I had given to her at the airport. Mama gladly hands it over and we high-five over the victory.

I race down the bleachers, and in one fell swoop, grab the top of the fence and sail over it in what I have to admit is a pretty cool, rock star-like move.

"Fooorrest!" "I'm sooo glad you're back, doll!" Heather proclaims as D.J. lights upon us rapidly.

"Let's go, Heather," D.J. commands, his angry dragon breath still steaming out of his mouth.

"Go jump in the lake," Heather snaps. "You almost cost us the game. What a loser!" she calls out as she turns her back on him.

Heather reaches for my arm. "Forrest, you look amazing. I lovvvve the leather!" She coos, stroking my jacket. She's ready to bask in the attention it will bring her as the pretty girl on the arm of the dude who rocked on the same stage as KISS.

"Hey, Heather. This is for you," I declare, placing the KISS backstage pass around her neck. "You're gonna make a *great groupie* someday."

"Are you *kidding me*? FORREST, GET BACK HERE!" Heather wails like a spoiled child. She realizes the gift is meant to mock her. She is suddenly at a loss for sarcastic words.

"Hey, Heather, you have D.J.," I yell back over my shoulder as I start to jog to the middle of the field. "You two deserve each other!" I add, with a dismissive wave of my hand over my head.

I can't wait to congratulate my best friend for the game of his life. I run up behind Kyle and give him a "bro-slap" on his butt pads. He turns to face me and bursts out with laughter. "Oh, dude, Forrest...I thought that was your MAMA!" He grabs me by the shoulders and shakes my spent body.

"Maaan...that was sooo wrong!" I protest. My numb brain is too tired to think of a comeback line. I can tell by the ornery grin on Kyle's face that he's thrilled to get me back for the Mrs. Smith comment from weeks ago. Tonight, all victories are his.

"Congratulations, dude. What an epic game!" I exclaim as I exhale.

"Thanks, man. You know you're part of this, too. You helped get us here, Forrest." Kyle assures.

"Oh, I know, man. Right now you need to enjoy the glory. You deserve it, Kyle," I return.

"I hear you and your band killed it in Sweden, dude," Kyle yells over the school fight song.

"It was incredible! I'll tell ya all about it later. I gotta go say hi to someone."

I'm distracted by Sophie waving her drumsticks at me. I can't wait to see her pretty face up close and personal.

"I'll see ya in the locker room, dude," I promise Kyle.

My heart swells with anticipation. I'm on a mission for a hug. I think to myself, *How adorable Sophie looks in her band uniform,* as I grab her up into my arms—"my little band geek!" Her clumsy, furry, band hat tips forward like it did at the pep assembly, almost covering her angel eyes. I hug her and the hat tilts back, giving me the perfect opportunity to sneak a first kiss. We hover several feet off the ground for a few seconds, before drifting like a falling feather back to earth.

"What about Heather?" She asks, pushing me back. Sophie's warm breath puffs delicately from her perfect mouth.

"Sophie...I'm so sorry. I should've broken up with Heather weeks ago. She's spoiled rotten, and definitely more suited to a guy like D.J.," I apologize. "Besides, I bet he'll give her more compliments for her daily vanity list than I ever did."

We grin at each other and hug tightly one more time. I rub her shoulders to help her warm up. I feel my heart race through my button-down shirt as I draw the courage to ask her out. I still think it's funny that I can play in front of thousands of people without stage fright, but hugging sweet Sophie makes me weak in the knees. I inhale, drawing the sharp night air deep into my lungs.

"Sophie, would ya like to come over to my house and chill for awhile tonight? No big deal. My parents always order pizza, and we can just hang out or something?" I ask sheepishly, with travel-weary eyes. It's becoming hard for me to separate reality from a dream at this point. I'm so jet lagged and emotionally spent. I sure don't want to wake up now if this is a dream. *Just stay asleep, Forrest*, I think in my delirious mind.

Sophie looks at me with her endearing sideways glance. "Only if we can watch movies and listen to music," she returns slyly. She clasps her soft, cold hand in mine.

"That's definitely a deal," I smile, nodding my head in relief. I can feel her hand warm quickly as we touch. I smile wider knowing now this isn't just a dream. I don't even need Jake here to pinch me!

She wants to watch movies and listen to music! I

marvel happily. *Where has this amazing girl been all my life?*

Sophie and I start for the field house when I hear a familiar riff. It's my band's song, "Rocket," blaring from the P.A. system above the home bleachers. I look back to the stands and see my mom and dad smiling. Their index fingers point in the air above their heads signifying the number one. I look back to Sophie with a puzzled expression.

"Didn't your folks tell you, Forrest?" She asks, raising her voice above the song. "'Rocket' just made it to the top ten on the charts! Your sister Megan told me before the game. Your parents must've wanted to surprise you!"

I grab my curls, pushing them away from my face. I'm simply stunned by the news. Our song is a bullet! I turn once again to the football field. My teammates are rocking out to my tune. Even cowboy Coach Bryan is jamming to the music with an imaginary air guitar. Knowing him though, it's probably an "air banjo."

"Oh, man…this is *amazing*!" I exclaim.

Standing on the fifty-yard line, I look up at the clear night sky full of tiny, brilliant stars. I take a deep breath and say a silent prayer of thanks. A wonderful family, great friends, a girl who understands me, and a hit song. What more could a teenage boy ask for?

Answer…NOTHING!

CHAPTER TWENTY THREE

The stadium is empty, except for Janitor Hank, who is sweeping up the empty popcorn boxes and sticky Coke cups. Mini orange and black plastic pom-poms lie strewn like beached jellyfish in the deserted bleachers.

The Tigers have won the coveted State Championship game, with a too-close-for-comfort score of thirty-three to twenty-seven. The students and town folk have taken their celebration to the local Pizza Hut, Snack Shack, and in true small town fashion, the Quick Trip parking lot. The red necks are wild tonight.

The assistant coach stays behind to lock up the field house, and a handful of marching band students are turning in their uniforms. The stadium lights still burn bright over the empty bleachers, hypnotizing the army of moths that swarm around the glaring globes.

Late as usual, Jake, Randy and Cody walk together through the abandoned ticket booth. The three exhausted rockers make their way to the chain link fence that encircles the quiet, empty football field. Jake holds two bags of Taco Bell, Randy carries sodas and candy bars, and Cody sports a giant, orange, very conspicuous "number one" foam finger.

The three boys had gone to the practice barn to unload their gear, and lit into an impromptu jam session. They're still jet-lagged from the time change between Sweden and the United States and, par for the course, the clueless rockers are late for the Ball once again.

"Duuude…where's the game, man?" Jake asks, as he wipes his greasy long hair away from his face.

"I think I saw an episode of *The Twilight Zone* where somethin' like this happened…only it was in an old, creepy house, and not at a football field," Randy whispers eerily.

"Oh, man…..I think we missed the *whole thing*. I guess Forrest was right—we *did* finally miss the boat!" declares Cody, as if he's in deep philosophical thought.

"But hey, at least we have snacks!" Randy calls out enthusiastically as he tears into a king size Butterfinger candy bar.

As they ponder their existence in the universe, the three confused rockers hear giggles echoing behind them. They turn toward the band room door to see a trio of gangly girls filing out toward them on the sidewalk. Instrument cases in hand, each of them sport a classic band-geek, puff-painted t-shirt.

The three young ladies walk toward the boys. Jake can see that the tallest of the three cuties has a KISS backstage pass hanging around her neck. It's the sacrificial pass that Heather had thrown down onto the sidelines in a temper tantrum. It's now a souvenir that will surely be treasured by the clarinet player forever.

Jake and Randy look at the bright-eyed girls and flash them the rock sign, while Cody holds up the big orange number one foam finger. The three marching band members return the rock sign, and grin widely at the boys, exposing a variety of braces and retainers.

"Duuuuude!" the rockers exclaim in unison. They high-five each other—Cody's giant foam finger whacks Randy right in the eye.

The two groups of teens couldn't have been more different, but as they sit together under the goal post and begin to talk, they're all pleasantly surprised to see just how much they have in common. The boys share their Taco Bell, candy bars and sodas. The diverse group of teens swaps stories about their favorite music videos, rock bands and live concerts.

The glaring stadium lights snap off, and the moth army retreats, but the group of music enthusiasts stay and talk for over an hour. Jake even asks one of the girls, named Parker, out for the following Saturday night. She accepts with a blush.

They decide on a concert and Taco Bell—a/k/a teen Nirvana.

It's on this night that each and every one of the deliriously tired members of Cellar Door Is Gone fully realize—BAND GIRLS ROCK!!

CHAPTER TWENTY FOUR

The week after the State Championship game, the boys and I all pitch in and buy Coach Bryan a brand new black felt cowboy hat. I also give Coach a baseball cap with the words "ROCK IT BIG ORANGE!" blazed in flaming letters. Coach says he'll wear it for the kick-off game next season if I'll work on writing a country song. I say it's a deal, and he squeezes my hand in a vice grip as we shake on it.

Heather and D.J. have officially started dating. She gets to ride in his pimped out Honda every day, and he gives her at least one compliment every hour. Their favorite activity is to sit at the mall food court eating Chinese food as they make fun of all the "losers." I was right. They are absolutely made for each other.

My band is set to leave for a two-week, East Coast radio tour, and we're going to be cruising in style. The record label has rented a tour bus for us, complete with X-box, satellite and a full kitchen. Randy is stoked for the "meals on wheels."

Kyle has been recruited by the Oklahoma Sooners. My dad is super excited, and purchased season tickets. When we're not traveling with the band, we'll be able to go watch Kyle play. I'm still going to miss my best bud, but I know he'll always be just a phone call away.

Megan has secured the honor of Valedictorian of her senior class, and received a scholarship to The University of Oklahoma, as well. Mom and Dad are so proud of her, and yes, so am I. Megan's also dating some "mystery dude." She's gone out with him a few times in the past couple of weeks on the down low. I'm protective of my sis and really want to meet the guy, but Megan seems particularly happy with him, so I'll just have to wait and see.

Today is Thanksgiving. My family and I have always helped out with our local church, delivering Thanksgiving meals to the shut-ins, the elderly, and anyone else who is in need. This year is no exception. I'm in awe as I survey at least eight hundred meals in plastic Wal-Mart bags stacked along the walls, waiting to be delivered. The delectable smell of succulent turkey and warm pumpkin pie waft through the air. It makes my mouth water. There will be plenty to eat later this afternoon at Aunt Carmen's, where my family will gather for our massive Thanksgiving feast.

I'm busy organizing the meals to be delivered when I spot the same two gossiping hens I had encountered in the doughnut shop weeks earlier. They're in rare form once again, shaking their heads and gossiping as though they're in the Country Cuts Salon downtown. They stand pointing at Mrs. Walton and Mr. Franklin, the kind elderly couple who found companionship in each other after the deaths of their spouses.

I cross over to Mr. Franklin and his sweetheart and greet them. "Happy Thanksgiving!" I smile, taking Mrs. Walton's frail hand.

"Oh, Happy Thanksgiving to you, too!" Mr. Franklin replies. "It's so good to see young people like you helpin' out in the community. You're a good egg, Forrest," Mr. Franklin says in a shaky voice.

"I'm glad to do it. I know I've been really blessed, too," I tell him humbly.

"Oh, honey, don't you know it," Mrs. Walton says, patting my hand gently.

I bid them "good day," and make my way back across the room. I'm feeling a little devilish right here in church, and just can't resist the chance to stir up the two blue-haired gossiping hens.

"Ladies! You look *beautiful* this morning...Happy Thanksgiving," I sing out boldly, mustering my most innocent smile.

The two women eye me up and down with shocked expressions and pull their shoulders back as though I might grab their pocketbooks and run.

"Uh...you, too," one of the plump women replies, cautiously.

"You ladies have a W-O-N-D-E-R-F-U-L holiday weekend," I call out, as though they're hard of hearing.

"Well, thank you, honey!" her surprised gossip-passing partner gushes. The two skeptics nod in approval. I turn to wink at Mr. Franklin and Mrs. Walton. They send a warm, knowing smile back to me.

"Kill em' with kindness," I whisper under my breath...as a matter of fact, I think that'll be the name of my next song.

My family and I load over fifty Thanksgiving meals into our vehicles and hit the streets of our little town. I'm always saddened by the condition of some of the homes where we deliver the meals. Even as tiny as our community is, there are still streets that I never drive down—streets that are lined with dilapidated houses, containing people in need.

Dad, Mama, Megan, and I pull up to a small, brick duplex. A scruffy, wire haired, mixed breed pup yaps loudly on the other side of the crooked fence as my family and I file down the cracked sidewalk. My heart sinks. I spot a miniature, rusting pink bicycle with a flat tire and broken handlebars propped up against the crumbling brick wall.

"Somebody's going to get a new bike from

Santa," Mama whispers. I know she and Dad will purchase a new bike and leave it on their porch Christmas day. I feel much better about the situation.

The doorbell is out of order, so I step up and knock three times at the door of the apartment located on the left of the complex.

"Who is it?" a gruff voice questions.

"Um...um...it's your Thanksgiving meals, sir," I stutter. I hear the metal scraping sound of the door chain sliding. The door creaks open slowly, reminding me of the scary movies from Red Box that Megan and I love to watch together. We aren't sure what is going to greet us from the other side.

"Hey, there!" I say officially. "We have four meals for your family," I continue.

As I hand them over, the recipient of the Thanksgiving dinners points at me.

"Duuuude! You're the lead singer of Cellar Door Is Gone!" he says in amazement.

"Yes...yeah, I am," I affirm, nodding my head.

"Hey, Junior...get out here, man. The lead singer of Cellar Door Is Gone is here, man!" the long-haired rocker yells over his shoulder. He flicks his lit cigarette onto the ground and stomps it out with Jesus sandals that are sandwiched over white crew socks.

I shake his hand and then Junior appears from the back of the tiny, dark apartment.

"I'm Justin Thomas, but everyone calls me J.T., and this here's Junior. We're brothers. Man, it is soooo cool to meet ya!" he says, shouting once again over his shoulder, this time for his wife to come join them.

"I can't believe it! We follow ya' in the paper and have yer CD," Junior continues. "You dudes'r great!"

"Well, thanks, man! It's great to meet you all," I reply, nodding my head. The brothers accept the meals with a heartfelt thank you, and hand them back to Junior's wife, Tiffany.

"Dude, how was it openin' fer KISS…when are y'all goin' on tour again?" J.T. inquires, rolling both questions together quickly.

"Oh, man, KISS was amazing!" I begin. I'm stoked for the conversation and the avid rockers hang on my every word. "We've got plans to go on a radio tour for a couple of weeks before Christmas, and our management's workin' on a tour after the first of the year. We're sooo ready to go," I explain with excitement that is contracted by the two enthusiastic fans.

"Man, that's just awesome, dude! Hey….can we get a pic with ya?" Junior asks.

"Sure, man…no problem. Do ya have a camera?" I inquire, stepping back onto the uneven sidewalk.

"Hey Tiff, hand me baby girl's little camera!" Junior calls out. He hands my mom a hot pink Barbie disposable camera.

"Okay," Junior instructs. "Just push this do-dad to take the picture. Then this here disc on the back, with the jaggedy edge, will take ya to the next one," he continues. Junior backs up and puts his arm around my shoulder. Mama knows how to use every camera known to man and gets tickled at his tutorial.

"All right. On three...say 'ROCK ON!'" Mama chimes as she holds up the camera.

J.T. suddenly spies Megan standing behind Dad. "Hey, young lady, aren't ya Forrest's sister?" He asks pointing in her direction.

"Yep, I sure am," Megan answers proudly.

"Well, by dang, then yer famous, too. Come get in the pic, girl!" J.T. calls out, motioning her over.

Megan bounds over and takes her place in the lineup. I'm grateful for his giving special treatment to Megan, and for the smiles that our visit brings to their faces. I take it all in—the radiant fall morning, the yipping Heinz 57 dog barking at the fence, and the plastic quacking sound of Mama advancing the film on the Barbie camera. It's all heartwarming.

I think about how the pictures are going to turn out—me smiling, Megan giggling, J.T.'s mullet blowing in the breeze, and Junior's eyes closed, while grinning from ear to ear.

As Mama snaps the last picture, we hear a honk from the street. Kyle sees us and waves enthusiastically, as he pulls his pickup truck parallel to the curb.

"Hey, man!" I greet him. I begin to make my way back down the sidewalk, but my journey is interrupted by Megan, who almost knocks me over as she comes darting by me in a flash.

I stop dead in my tracks, trying to figure out

where the fire is. I haven't seen Megan move this fast since Dad chased her around with a mousetrap, complete with deceased mouse.

My jaw goes slack as I witness my sister run to the driver side window of the truck and kiss my best friend. Yes—Megan kissed Kyle!

"Are you KIDDING meee!" I gasp. "REALLY?"

Kyle grins at me and shrugs his shoulders in an unsure manner. I know he's not sure how I'm going to react to the awkward situation.

"Yeah, man. Are you okay with this?" Kyle asks cautiously.

I shake my head and take a few slow steps toward Kyle's pickup. Reaching through his truck window, I give my buddy a hard, but harmless knuckle punch on the shoulder. I honestly have to laugh. I never, ever would have thought of this in a million years, but they actually make a kinda cute couple.

"Good luck with her, man—she's quite a handful!" I tease, still a state of shock.

Kyle is relieved by my response. We're already bros. Now, maybe we'll be future "bros-in-law."

It's all good.

Megan blows a non-sarcastic kiss to me as they pull away. "See you all at Aunt Carmen's! Love ya, bub!" *Wow.....my sis is growin' up!*

I jog back to my new buds, Junior and J.T. "Rock on, man. Happy Thanksgiving and God Bless!" I give the brothers each a fist bump.

"Yeah! Rock on, man. Go get em' on the tour and be safe, lil' dude!" Junior exclaims.

The two brothers stand with giddy, gap-toothed smiles. Junior gives me the thumbs up; J.T. gives me the rock sign.

I jump into my Chevy pickup, pull out my BlackBerry, and hit speed dial. "Hey, are ya ready?" I ask calmly, although filled with expectation. "Okay. I'm on my way to pick ya up. Aunt Carmen will be soooo glad to finally meet you. Love ya, Sophie!" I say, my voice a little more high-pitched than usual.

I feel content and complete. I put my truck in gear and pull out onto the antique brick streets that were laid by prisoners back in the old days. I roll down my windows and let the pure, crisp November air rifle through the cab.

I glance into the rearview mirror and almost don't recognize myself. My reflection reveals the shorter haircut that I had gotten the week before. Mama cried and saved my thick curly ponytail in a Ziploc bag. I now have rad "devil locks," with cool sharp side burns and shorter curls down the back of my neck. The girls at school and on Facebook are crazy for my makeover. Sophie loves it, too. It's different, but good—it was time for a change.

I slip on my Ray Ban aviators, and turn onto a bumpy, back country road. I'm off to pick up Sophie, who lives just two miles past Aunt Carmen's homestead. The brilliant autumn sun comes alive. Its rays dance like daytime fireflies, as it reflects over the lazy ripples in Aunt Carmen's pond. I honk at Mojo as I rumble past Aunt C's pasture. His ears prick up. He begins to race my truck down the barbed wire fence line. The majestic sorrel holds his head high. He flexes his muscles and morphs from a gallop into a dead, thirty-five mile an hour run. It's the perfect picture to describe how I know we both feel this very moment—free!!

Betty is buckled safely in the back seat keeping me company. I pull on my Joe's Tire ball cap, turn on KMOD and crank my stereo volume to max—there's no one here to tell me to turn it down. My calloused fingers begin to keep time on the well-worn, knuckle-indented leather steering wheel. I recognize the song playing within the first two beats. Even though it's a brand new single, I know each and every word by heart already. The song is "Sweet Goodbye," track number two from the debut album by a young, red dirt rock band called Cellar Door Is Gone, which hails from the Midwest—Cowtown, Oklahoma, to be exact.

~ROCK ON~

AUTHOR'S NOTE

This novel was inspired by the true life experiences of Forrest French, former lead singer/guitarist for teen rock band, Crooked X. The setting is real, but some characters are strictly products of the author's imagination. This novel in no way represents any of his former band members, their families, former management or professional representatives.

ACKNOWLEGMENTS

I would like to thank Monty, my hard working husband of 27 years, for allowing me the time to finally put my thoughts to paper, my daughters Jessica and Skylar for supporting my creative process and always looking out for their little brother, my mother who passed her passion for writing down to me, and my father for being one of Forrest's biggest fans from the day of his birth. Thank you to Eddie and Carolyn French for their positive feedback and constant love. Much appreciation to my sisters, Shannon and Faith, for believing in me and giving me constant comic relief, and to my wonderful community of Coweta, Oklahoma, Tulsa radio station KMOD, and attorneys at law, Mike Redman, Kenneth Freundlich and Walt and Mary Murray for their invaluable friendship and assistance with Forrest's musical ventures. I am forever grateful for the hospitality of MTV, The Dallas Cowboy football franchise, Brad Harris and The Cain's Ballroom, Red Bull, and my ancestor's home of Sweden, along with its beautiful people. Thank you to Jennet Grover, my lovely editor and mentor, who encouraged me with each step along the way, and helped me to bring my story to life. Thank you to Donna Font and Neverland Publishing for their philosophy of taking chances on first time authors, and making the process of publishing a book a most enjoyable, heartwarming experience. Last but not least, my biggest acknowledgment goes to my talented son Forrest, for inspiring me in this work and in my world each and every day by holding his family values close to his heart and his faith in God above all else.

Hailing from the small farming and ranching community of Coweta, Oklahoma, author and substitute teacher Jody French's love for working with and relating to teens, as well as her passion for her son's music, inspired her to write her first novel for young adults, *Red Dirt Rocker*.

In addition to writing and traveling, Jody loves to spend time with her husband, three children and three grandchildren. Rumor has it that some of her writing has been accomplished with a grandbaby on her lap.

Jody is a member of the Tulsa writer's group, Tulsa Inkslingers, as well as the online group, Scribophile.

13016649R00103

Made in the USA
Charleston, SC
12 June 2012